BLACK
SOULS

GIOACCHINO
CRIACO

—

Translated from the ~~~~~~~~~~~~~~~~~~~~~~ ey

SOHO
CRIME

Copyright © 2008 Rubbettino Editore
English translation copyright © 2019 Hillary Gulley

This edition published in agreement with
Piergiorio Nicolazzini Literary Agency (PNLA)

First published in English in 2019 by
Soho Press, Inc.
227 W 17th Street
New York, NY 10011

Library of Congress Cataloging-in-Publication Data

Criaco, Gioacchino, 1965– author. | Gulley, Hillary, translator.
Black souls / Gioacchino Criaco
translated from the Italian by Hillary Gulley.
Other titles: *Anime nere*. English

ISBN 978-1-64129-128-6
eISBN 978-1-61695-998-2

I. Title
PQ4903.R53 A8513 2019 853'.92—dc23 2018040584

Interior design by Janine Agro

Printed in the United States of America

10 9 8 7 6 5 4 3 2 1

BLACK
SOULS

Much—too much—blood
has been spilled by and has flowed from the children of the forest,
brothers uselessly and stupidly divided.
If only God and the Gods could placate the warrior spirit of their souls,
and drive away the demon that possesses them.

CONTENTS

BLACK
SOULS

We walked at a clip, wresting ourselves from the damp embrace of the heather and ferns. He marched ahead of me, while I trailed behind like a dogsled. We had already milked the goats and, after closing them into the fold and storing their milk, in the first shadows of nightfall we set off, crossing the mountain and leaving behind our view of one sea in pursuit of another. The delivery of the swine would take place many miles away.

It had been drizzling for days. A heavy camouflage jacket, Spanish military issue, kept the water from drenching my shirt and pants. The steam from my body exited the jacket in puffs, and through the pockets, which opened to the inside, I kept making sure that my AK-47 was dry, and that the safety lever remained on, and not in the full or semi-automatic position. The shock of cold metal added to the adrenaline that was already in my veins.

We traversed forests of holm oak, low and dense,

invaded by thorny broom that sometimes won their struggle against our clothing and marked our flesh; the narrow rows of pines, with their branches low and dry, constantly sought out our eyes, forcing us to lower our heads so our cap visors could defend us against their onslaughts; forests of towering, majestic larch trees, whose soft needles concealed deep holes dug by the wild boars, tested the flexibility and stability of our ankles, and one misstep was all it took to end up slung over the strong shoulders of a companion—assuming there was one to come to the rescue. Immense beech trees claimed the flatlands, which were scattered with leaves that produced a deafening crunch in the silent forest.

After we reached the summit and began our descent, the vegetation repeated itself in reverse. Even in daylight, such a hike would have been unthinkable—suicide—for someone with untrained eyes, with its tangled brush, perilous rocks, impulsive torrents, malicious cliffs, and barbed wire fences.

He was in symbiosis with the apparently savage wilderness, merged with it wholly and a part of it, one more of its essential elements: the mountain, which rejects hostility, accepted him, and in return he loved it more than any other thing in this world.

It was his belief that he and the mountain hated only two things: oak trees and swine, both terrible for the environment. The oaks made the soil dry and desert-like, and its fruits nourished the swine, which in turn destroyed the forests, embankments, mushrooms, crops, and pastures.

He knew every step, every tree, brook, cliff, shelter, and pitfall as only a native of these parts could. He had been born and raised here. He had gone away for some time, but the mountain inevitably reclaimed him. Whoever was born of it would die there. And there were only two ways to die: from exhaustion or a lead bullet. It was nearly impossible to escape both fates.

The man in question was my father.

A typical product of this land—thickset, strong, tough. Hardened and fragile at the same time. Above all, determined to resist the rule of law or morals at any cost.

Together, we devoured the road that would take us to the swine, our land's sustenance and poison.

It was still dark when we arrived. We swept the area in a series of concentric circles that contracted as we went. Not a soul. Only nocturnal animals for company. We sat down on two large rocks downhill from the guardrail that divided the rest stop from the highway. And we waited.

From time to time a noise would shake the silence of night and two headlights would pierce the darkness. Only passing cars. And we would go back to waiting.

After a few hours we heard a different sort of rumble. A truck slowed to a roll and stopped. A door opened and shadows scurried along the guardrail and crouched low to the ground. The truck went on its way.

A few seconds later, the silence and darkness took over again.

I could sense their odors, their thoughts. They weren't afraid; they knew we were expecting them. Then my father's clipped, dry whistle dissolved any possible fear: they'd done it, they were safe. The weight of their misdeeds had now been shifted onto my father's robust shoulders.

Tense, I stepped into the open. The swine walked toward us calmly, upright. I had hoped he would arrive shrunken and imploring, so I wouldn't be forced to show him any respect or mercy. Instead, he held his shoulders back, his head high. He didn't fear us, or so it appeared. And his appearance also said that the most important thing, his family, was now far from him and safe. He wasn't afraid to face us.

Trouble was guaranteed, I thought.

We approached each other in silence. My father took Luciano's hand, placed it on his shoulder, and led him a safe distance from the road. He did the same with Luigi. Then we took the swine from either side and escorted him over. We would leave at the first light of dawn. And when the time came, my father turned to the swine and spoke to him in a low voice, with a hint of sweetness, explaining that it would be a long journey on foot, that he would remove his handcuffs, that they would stop whenever he felt tired, that he could eat and drink at his every request, and that my father would carry him on his back through the most dangerous stretches. If he didn't cooperate, however, he would be dragged, forced to crawl along the ground.

The swine nodded and we departed.

We marched at a pace. And after a few hours my father decided that the others needed to rest.

My friends and I did not speak, slapping one another's backs as we came to a halt. I dropped my backpack, took out a hot plate, and made coffee. I distributed chocolate and biscotti and, in that forest of oaks bathed in the light April rain, I observed the strange company lazing on the ground, waiting for the moka pot to perfume the air with its sputters and spurts. The scene was tranquil but for the heavy hood that covered the swine's head.

The coffee bubbled up. I poured it into paper cups and passed them around. Luciano was in ecstasy, this was his favorite part of being on the mountain. Whenever he went up he took long hikes for the sheer pleasure of tiring himself out so he could lie against the trunk of a tree, sip the coffee I made for him and, finally, light one of his trademark cigarettes; he always tried to draw out the moment for as long as possible, to savor it even more. After the night he had spent on the truck and the long hike, he was happy to be living life, his cigarette between his lips.

We drank the coffee and ate the chocolate. When

Luciano languidly tried to light another cigarette—his third—my father snatched it from his lips and we resumed our journey.

The swine walked peacefully, never asking for water or food, and so we arrived earlier than planned. My father set out ahead of us, accelerating his pace, and upon our arrival we found steaming plates of ricotta and whey with toasted bread on the side. We ate in abundance, and even the swine seemed to appreciate the local dish. My father kept guard while we four, still in our coats, lay on the broom mat by the heat of the gas stove.

A few hours later my father woke us up. The hostage was gone; my father had already taken him to his lodging, he said.

We hid our firearms and our camouflage, we changed, we helped to milk the goats, and then set off in the car down the curving potholed dirt road that led into town.

The next morning, as always, we took the 6:30 bus to the city, where we sat at our desks at the high school for five hours at a stretch to attend lessons.

In those times it seemed normal to me that a man could be called a swine, the word the shepherds of the Aspromonte used for the many hostages we hid away in those intricate woods.

To earn their name, the *shepherds*, who owned the

mountains and everything in them, kept watch over the goats, the only noble beasts that deserved to graze at such harsh altitudes. The goats were companions and friends.

A true shepherd would spit on sheep, even his own— idiot flock animals; he feared the cows, with their superhuman senses; and he raised one pig each year, damaging as pigs were to the land, keeping it apart from the other animals and feeding it only whey and scraps. It was an odious beast, but the meat it yielded was essential for enduring the harsh winters.

And, resuming ancient practices that survived in the stories recounted by the elders, a few shepherds would keep a second, secret pigsty in addition to the one near their goat enclosure, perfectly camouflaged in the thick of the forest, for filthy but more profitable livestock. Necessary for the economic development that they had been led to believe was on its way.

That's how things were back then, for many and also for me.

And for some years this was my father's real trade, and mine.

At the start of spring, we would build a new pigsty a few miles from the fold. We'd hold a hostage there for four or five months during the mildest season. Once the ransom was paid, we would return the hostage, who was then released in a completely different area.

Generous as he was with all the poor, God had blessed

my father with seven children. First me, then five girls, and finally another boy.

As a child, my father had been a shepherd's apprentice—really a shepherd's servant. After marrying, he moved away and sent every last lira back home. When he had finally saved enough to buy his own herd, he returned to his mountains.

I can remember a zinc tub from my childhood where each week we would take turns bathing in the same bathwater; we ate pasta or potatoes in a light broth of thinned tomato paste, our clothes were patched and always the same, we wore open sandals in both summer and winter, and we shared a bed with an iron bar in the middle, which I can still feel in the center of my back.

Luciano's childhood was just like mine, minus a father. He'd never known his own, riddled with buckshot before he was born.

Luigi, the youngest of ten children, with a father who was married to all the taverns in town, had also found in us the family he'd never had.

Childhoods like ours were common to almost all of our peers, yet not all of them ripened into the lethal fruit we did; quiet destroyers of lives, our violence discreet, we would become the most dangerous kind of people.

Outside of our loyalties everyone was an enemy,

expendable. With one another we were affectionate, thoughtful, almost sweet.

Our childhood memories had created us—or we were genetically predisposed. Our violence inflicted pain in places and on people who thought themselves safe from us.

By the age of nineteen we had stolen, robbed, kidnapped, and killed. In a world we rejected because it was not our own, we took anything and everything we wanted.

That nocturnal trek forever changed our lives and those of so many others. We had long since embarked on a road to hell, and this was the last in a series of many wrong turns. The hostage we went to collect was not part of the usual service we provided for the mafia. That swine we claimed from the mists of the Po Valley was ours alone.

THE
CHILDREN
OF THE
FOREST

Three normal students. Or so we seemed.

At school, as with everything in life, Luigi was a tagalong; I got by, sticking somewhere in the middle; and Luciano was the classic brainiac, with no topic he hadn't explored or book he hadn't read.

Three good boys, and not because we pretended to be; we had always been good, polite, never arrogant. But our world, on the other hand, began and ended with the three of us: we had been born and raised in the same wrinkle of humanity, a neighborhood block of sixteen families, about eighty souls, known as the Aurora because of the street that cut through its middle. We had stuck together through preschool, elementary school, middle school, high school, and so it would be in the future, we had sworn it. Nothing would ever divide us.

In high school they snubbed us for months, for years. Why did these shepherds' children bother studying past middle school? That's what everyone thought. In the end, even our classmates accepted us, because with time, people can get used to anything.

But we didn't think like them, children of professionals or the middle class. Our breakfasts, bus passes, books, clothes, entertainment, schooling, we paid for it all ourselves. We could have ended up slaving away for a pittance in some mechanic's workshop, or a barbershop, or under a master mason or, worst case, a shepherd.

We'd had a plan for ourselves since childhood. We had other ambitions.

Everyone knew there was an old gunsmith in the city whose only requirement was cash. We put together some cash with a few petty thefts, burgling people's homes or little shops, and arrived at Cavalier Attilio Fera, the gunsmith in question, with seven hundred thousand lire. We left with a legendary Colt Cobra 38-caliber Special and an equally mythical Beretta 7.65-caliber, model 70 with an automatic ejector.

So our quest for money began, along with the realization of our dreams.

The only thing at which Luigi excelled over everyone else was driving; we soon learned to hotwire cars, so we always had one somewhere, stashed in an alley or behind a bush. At least once a month we'd leave our three school desks empty to familiarize ourselves with places like post offices in the suburbs, small banks in the countryside, municipal treasuries, and goldsmiths.

We had more clothes now, and mixed up what we wore from day to day, dressing like the others or better, while at home the whole family's diet improved and I got a bed all to myself.

When I brought money home for the first time, my mother wept the whole day as if she were in mourning; my father bowed his head, didn't speak for a week, and eventually took to keeping swine.

In those years, in addition to the infamous kidnappings, there were the lesser-known detentions of small-scale land-owners that lasted a few days or a month at most, and which offered very little profit in proportion to their risks. But for those who had nothing, a few million lire was a lot, or everything.

My father started going out to bars in the evening, something he'd never done before. After a while, random friends of his would stop by our goat pasture. Strange people. Men who spoke a language all their own, ancient, mysterious, and incomprehensible, making mention of skilled, capable, talented people.

An unknown world suddenly opened up to me, a world of good-natured caresses and wet kisses, a deadly embrace. A world that, later on, would make me want to vomit at the mere thought of it.

At first I didn't notice the dark side. We fell in love with these people, my father and I. Only Luciano knew better; he couldn't stand them. He tried to warn us about how petty they were, how deceitful. But in the end he followed my lead, as he always did.

Those guys, as Luciano called them, were a constant presence in our lives and our fold for years. Copious eating and drinking at our expense became a regular event.

Three or four times they brought us hostages to guard, which they would send for when they were to be freed; our poor new friends had so many people to provide for—sad widows, jailed conspirators, fugitives—there was never much profit left over to share with us. So they'd leave us a few million lire and promise the next time would be better.

Then we'd recommence the grand feasts, we'd embrace and kiss and pledge our eternal friendship and mutual assistance, and we'd make even more deals together. We spent our every profit on festivities, on obligations, because the godfathers had to make their rounds, presenting themselves at one wedding after the next with bulging envelopes.

With *those guys* around, people began to stay in the fold, people whom we referred to as *shadows*, wanted men, *fuiùti*, the vanished, the fugitives; there was always someone to look after. Generally, they were good boys of a certain innocence that the godfathers, *those guys*, had managed to get caught up in trouble, poor souls who had only been trying to leave their dark, stuffy houses to clear their heads in the mountains.

Unable to stand the hardship and the solitude, they never

lasted long. Many of them ended up in jail, dragged out from behind the cabinets in their village homes; others took refuge in large cities in the North or abroad, and many others were found lying in a ditch.

Most of the shadows that passed through the fold forgot about us shepherds, but some retained a deep affection for us, and of these the more fortunate would send something our way.

Among the shadows who had not forgotten us was Stefano Bennaco, a jocular thirty-year-old kid who had been saddled with a life sentence for a kidnapping gone wrong. He eventually found refuge in the Basque Country; he also loved the mountains, and of our transient guests, he was the one who went on to do the best for himself. Through his cousin he would send us anything that could be of use in the woods: backpacks, tents, camouflage, boots, fishing rods, bows, field lamps, camping cots. We had to build a small shed to contain all the gear.

There were two ways men became *shadows*: either because there were pending matters with the law or because of a problem to be settled with other private parties. If blood was then spilled, the shadow became either a "black soul" or a *tingiùto*, blacklisted, depending on whether they were expected to emerge from the conflict as victors, in the first case, or as victims.

Of the shadows who stayed with us during the war, I can remember two in particular: a *tingiùto* called Donato Porcino and a black soul by the name of Sante Motta.

Poor Donato's father had refused to grant his daughter's hand in marriage to a local crook, a *malandrino*, and the latter expressed his grievances by taking the woman by force and killing his would-be father-in-law. Donato swore revenge and was a *tingiùto* from that day forth.

He found doors were closed to him, even at the houses of friends and close relatives. Knowing that his father had been my mother's godfather, he appeared at our house one night. We hid him in the mountains for months, unbeknownst to anyone, while trying to convince him to leave the region for a time; we wanted to send him to our friend in the North, another shadow. He insisted on going to his godfather in a neighboring village, a respectable person who would surely help him. We led him through the mountains and, when he was in sight of his godfather's fold, he hugged us and thanked us with sincerity. I tried to plead with him one last time, offering to travel with him, but he replied that a man doesn't bring trouble to his friends.

He was never seen again, thanks to his godfather.

The other shadow, Sante Motta, was the illegitimate son of an old *malandrino* who had lived a blessed life, with legitimate children born of his Christian marriage whom he dressed in expensive cotton clothes and sent off to school, sparing only what was left over for Sante. When times changed, and new and more ruthless godfathers came to replace the fat and lazy men of honor, Don Santoro got his lead bullet and met the prince of darkness. His legitimate heirs sold everything and moved far away to enjoy the fruits of the old man's thirty years of dirty dealings. Only Sante heard the calling of the blood, and by force of gunfire he assumed his father's place.

For years Sante led an almost hermetic life, trusting few. During his time in hiding, in addition to sowing death, he accumulated a great deal of wealth, being among the first to discover what could be had from drug money.

From Sante we inherited many things, good and bad: the AK-47 and the CZ-75, the Russian submachine gun and the pistol from the Czechoslovakian army, ultramodern weapons for that time and place, where the most anyone had ever seen was a Beretta or Franchi 12-gauge double-barrel; he opened our eyes to the *malandrini* and marred our souls by teaching us to kill. His mother, war widow of a foreign shepherd, lived in the country of her late husband in a land that overlooked the sea opposite ours and had five sons with five different men; she was the elder sister of my father, who had never forgiven her for her conduct—a product of poverty—and who had withdrawn his sympathies, bad blood he carried to his grave.

But Sante came to us because we were his blood. On account of his sister, my father was not, nor could he have ever become, a *malandrino* himself; at most he'd provide his services to the mafia.

Older folks referred to illegitimate children as mules, and said that God made them physically identical to their natural fathers to expose their sin to the world, that these children spent their lives proving they were better and more worthy of affection than legitimate children. And so it was.

But contrary to what everyone believed, Sante told us that his father had sent for him often, had been affectionate with him, and had shared all his wisdom, more than with his other children. The old boss knew he could be killed anytime. He told Sante, "If they get me, do something about it only if you want, and only do what you can do yourself without help. When you hit you have to do it before they know you're coming; once you've gone down that road there is no return, because sooner or later an orphan will appear in your path, unless you have the courage to wean them from their mother's milk. If you need to hide out, go to people who are considered to be of little value, they'll feel ennobled and will never betray you. Avoid the *malandrini*, today they represent the cancer of our land. In their discussions you'll find them wise, honorable, loyal, but in reality from the top down they are almost always cheaters, traitors, informants, and *tragediatori*."

And Sante explained what a *tragediatore* was, according to his father's definition: when a *malandrino* had an enemy he didn't consider to be dangerous, he'd shoot him and do nothing to hide it. If his enemy was dangerous, he needed to be eliminated without consequences; it was therefore necessary to find someone else who would pull the trigger or who could take the blame. The *malandrino* would wait, sometimes for years, until the victim in question had a fresh conflict, during which he'd immediately strike; the relatives, blinded by grief, would unleash their hatred on the most recent enemy, forgetting the old grudges of the deceased, and then all remaining parties would annihilate each other, to the delight of the *tragediatore*. When this sort of scenario wasn't possible, the *tragediatore* would circulate some bait, and when it found the right subject, the latter would make the hit; some unlucky dupe, convinced he'd freed the world of a crook, would find himself with a smoking gun in his hand and naturally take the fall.

With those teachings in mind, Sante hid his hatred and pain when his father died, even skipping his funeral, playing the part of an abandoned mule. He went on with his usual life for a time; then, with the excuse that he was off to seek his fortune, he said goodbye to everyone—including his father's murderers—and left.

A few years later he returned, armed with a machine gun, and made four hits in a single day, another the next day, and one more the day after that. Within a month his ten targets were gone. He returned quietly and safely to the North, where he made his money, and every two or three months he'd come back to refresh the memory of his potential enemies.

One misty winter's morning, when Sante was already famous in those lands and both my father and I were experts in our respective activities, he appeared at our fold with a Kalashnikov on one shoulder and a caliber 9 in his belt. He said, "Uncle, I need to stay here for a few days." My father offered him some warm ricotta and made up the bed. And not out of fear.

Every two or three months Sante would come, don his work clothes and work hard, maybe harder than my father. He spoke little, stayed the week, took care of business, and left; as soon as we heard he'd arrived, Luciano, Luigi, and I would promptly set aside our schooling and looting for a trip to the mountains. Sante had become our God.

He always set us straight, pointing out how much the lives of our *malandrino* friends had improved, as new cars started to circulate and the first big buildings went up, while they did nothing but complain. Meanwhile the shepherds who helped them were beginning to get a taste of life in prison on Asinara.

Our love for our "friends" vanished and gave way to a bitter hatred. With Sante by our side, we found the strength to distance ourselves from the mafia.

Slowly, slowly, my father began to break away. Those guys tried to draw us back in with their tall tales, but they reluctantly understood the party was over, absorbed the blow and, with rancor in their bodies, moved on to other goat pastures. Still, their stench had invaded our homes, our beds, our hearts; Sante promised us that when the time was right, he'd give us a big job to do. My father went back to his goats, and we left his mountain retreat and returned to town.

We should have been more cautious: our old friends were watching us now that we had given them the boot. We'd learned that protecting ourselves against them was more important than watching out for the police; their livelihood depended on their control over us, as if it were a function they'd been granted by law. Every crime they learned about and which they hadn't committed themselves was swiftly connected to a guilty party.

We took care—especially with Luigi, who was a talker by nature—to keep our business hidden. We stopped going into town. But in spite of my and Luciano's efforts, someone caught on. We had recently paid a visit to a nice watchmaker, and Luigi had insisted on keeping what we'd believed was a very simple watch, promising us that he would never wear it in public. But he couldn't resist.

Luigi came home late one evening as I was going to bed; he was wound up—and wearing his watch, I noticed—about some card game at the bar.

"You were at the bar? Were you wearing your watch?"

"I'll explain later, this is too important."

He'd been playing cards, he said, and had gotten up to go to the bathroom. As he was coming out, he ran into the director of the post office, accountant Turi D'Ascola, who was a great gambler, womanizer, and judge of character—or so they said. The accountant, cursing his bad luck in the game, was in a rage so blind he nearly didn't see Luigi. He let it slip that if he weren't such an honest state official he'd go home, get the keys to the post office, and swipe from the safe those hundred million lire that were awaiting transport the following day.

We'd always been careful never to do any jobs in our town, but in those days, and for three eighteen-year-old kids, that kind of opportunity was irresistible. So we found ourselves camped out behind a hedge waiting for the return of the accountant, who, without too much resistance—albeit at gunpoint—led us inside his house to retrieve the keys to the post office.

Luigi and Luciano stayed back to keep the accountant's wife and daughter company. I left by car with Turi D'Ascola. In half an hour I was back with the accountant and the money. We closed the hostages in the bathroom and, happy and incredulous at our easy luck, we sped away.

We hid the loot and in the morning went to school as usual. We tried to reproach Luigi for having gone against our recommendations but were too pleased with ourselves; and so, in the end, we went to the Valenciano to celebrate.

In the city, there were two places to lose your virginity, in the Baracche district or at the Valenciano. The Baracche district was a shantytown where the mature and foul-mouthed women worked; in a tangle of cats and sewers in the open air boys became men with whores who carried on heated arguments with their pimps and regulars while they worked. You were always left wondering whether the soggy thing you'd felt had been part of the female anatomy or, more likely, their torn stockings, which they often neglected to remove.

Five thousand lire—which included a case of the clap—and people went home happy.

The Valenciano, on the other hand, was a legendary hotel where well-heeled locals made love to exotic and beautiful foreign women. Twenty thousand lire a shot, a gentleman's price.

When our pockets were full, we'd present ourselves to the concierge, who was used to seeing us and often granted us an encore. Even the women seemed happy to be with three handsome boys instead of the vicious old men and their noisy hernias.

When our euphoria wore off we told Luigi not to change his habits for a while and to continue to frequent the bar, as it turned out he'd been doing, we discovered, for months.

In the evening the countryside was in turmoil. A big hit, professional stuff, hundreds of millions of lire, those were the rumors. The *malandrini* chewed salt and cursed the Madonna of the Mountain.

It was also said that poor accountant D'Ascola, due to

the fright of having six guns pointed at his head—because three bandits had held down his house and three more had dragged him to the post office—had fallen ill and was in a feverish state of confusion. After such an incredible trauma it was doubtful he would be able to return to work, given that he was already so old and close to retirement.

The next day we read the extensive report by the local correspondent in the *Gazzetta del Sud*: the morning before the event, the van used to distribute pension cash had suffered a mechanical failure at the start of its route. They couldn't repair it right away, so they decided to leave the money in the safe at the post office under D'Ascola's direction, postponing the remaining deliveries until the following day. Investigative sources had expressed their doubts, to no small degree, about the coincidence of the breakdown; the theory held that disloyal employees at the central office had plotted with the bandits, in league, of course, with the local underworld. The crushing loss amounted to one hundred and fifty million lire.

Now we were the ones chewing salt, because I was sure I had taken everything in that safe, but we were fifty million short of the figure cited in the paper.

We soon figured it out. Turi D'Ascola had a diabolical mind.

The accountant never went back to work, but retired early. With his leaving bonus he bought a vineyard to which he devoted himself entirely; he began to appear at the bar in the evenings again, but he no longer played cards, claiming he couldn't concentrate and contenting himself with watching the others play instead.

He ran into Luigi by the bathroom again, looked at him with a spark in his eye and asked the time, leaving Luigi so uncertain as to how to interpret the question that the accountant flashed his own silver pocket watch, a gift from the state for his forty years of service.

To top it off, D'Ascola whispered, "Your father must have saved hard to buy you that Rolex on your wrist."

Devil of an accountant, he had studied Luigi for months, how he dressed, how much he lost at cards, and when the Lord broke the delivery van he took it as a sign and immediately made his move; he brought fifty million lire to his house, cast the bait and waited for us in front of the garden, sure as the sunrise that we would show. And he secured for himself a more serene retirement.

Our old friends scratched their heads for months and eventually gave up, convincing themselves that it had been the work of out-of-towners.

In fact, they'd been duped on their own turf by three kids and an old scammer.

We widened the house. I now shared an entire room with only my little brother. The girls wept with joy when they found themselves sleeping in a room with five neat beds all in a row and a huge wardrobe where my mother began to store their clothes. This is basically all we'd wanted, a life of human beings and not of beasts. The girls wept harder when they saw the steaming water shoot from the showerhead and a shelf full of perfumed toiletries; we could say goodbye to the zinc tub. They were so happy that all five of them took our little brother and groomed him like a pig at Christmastime. In the evening they pampered my father and competed to see who could cut his nails, which were deformed by fifty years of hard work. He looked at me for an eternal instant before letting himself be kissed by the girls. I could have died in that moment with the certainty that my life had meant something. And, with the money from our small jobs, he made life better for that whole wrinkle where we three friends had been raised, two yellow barracks opposite each other with space for sixteen families.

The hit on the post office became an instant legend throughout the region and represented a turning point in our criminal careers. Until then we'd been poor boys trying to escape misery, believing that we had a right to a different future. Anything could have gotten in our way. From that day on, however, we had the conviction that we would be able to build our own destiny; at first, all we wanted was some cash, but from that point onward we aspired to be downright rich. We were destined to reach unimaginable heights, but if we'd known what else was in store for us, we never would have pursued them.

We were just entering our final year of high school, and that million-lire heist had shattered our inhibitions. We became voracious birds of prey. Our monthly hits became weekly, and the pressure was mounting. We needed to collect as much money as possible so we could enroll in university and move to Milan; we wanted to arrive in comfort, not as peasants.

During our graduation year we spent every Sunday in the mountains at my father's fold, which had become a paradise now that the *malandrini* were gone. I loved to milk the goats, to feel the tickle of their tails on my face. I was becoming like my father—I knew every part of the mountain, I took endless walks. Ever since our livelihood had ceased to depend on milk and meat, the mountains had become beautiful to me.

The countryside was a vast expanse of territory, all mountains. The migrations had swept up most of the shepherds, who took blue-collar jobs in Germany, Switzerland, Belgium, Turin, or Milan. There were fewer and fewer families of breeders, the pastures were ample and the mountains free, abandoned by the landowners.

Each shepherd chose his pasture in agreement with the others, and this became his kingdom. My father had two folds, the summer fold at the highest peak and the winter fold in the most protected valley in the foothills. One was at a height of 6500 feet above sea level, the other zero, though it was a good distance from the coast. He had woods of firs, oaks, beeches, wild pear trees; he had pinewoods, expanses of broom, fields of heather, tangles of holm oaks and brambles.

And now that our pockets were full, in the absence of anxiety I regarded those mountains with joy and even found pleasure in them.

In the summer we took backpacks, tents, sleeping bags, shotguns, and fishing rods, loaded up food, and roamed everywhere. It was like a long party, starting in the morning with fishing, when we'd fill the plastic containers with crickets to use for bait and place them at the edges of the waterfalls, casting long lines into the ponds that formed at the foot of the deep cliffs, and filling our baskets with huge brown and rainbow trout.

After fishing, we'd plunge into the frigid water completely naked, bake under the sun and shoot the shit, sparing ourselves any hard topics.

As always, Luciano took care of the cooking, preparing sauce with flaked trout and tomatoes, more trout roasted on the grill, and bruschetta with oil, tomatoes, garlic, and chili peppers. We ate and drank until we were stuffed. Coffee was my specialty.

After a healthy nap, we'd forage for the mushrooms that popped up like clockwork after every summer rain. We collected them gingerly, placing them in wicker baskets so they could release their spores onto the ground, allowing more to grow—the delectable Caesar's mushrooms, which sprouted like ripe persimmons among the mountain stones, and the parasol mushrooms, with their nutty flavor.

At dusk we waited for the hares and wild boars to come out to feed, then we would grill them when the hunt was fruitful, and in the middle of the night we'd walk arm in arm, howling at the wolves that were out hunting wild goats. In those times we could feel how much we needed each other. We loved one another dearly, and Luciano gave me proof of this his whole life, since I was the only person he had in this world—besides his poor mother, who would soon abandon him.

At night we hunted dormice, illuminated on the oaks under our large gas lamps, cleaned them with ash, and threw them in the ragù for our spaghetti.

We could survive months in the woods without wanting for a single thing.

When the heat became unbearable we'd spend our afternoons asleep in our spaceship. At the foot of the mountains, there was a fork produced by the confluence of two streams; just where the torrents met there was a huge white stone that the water had brought to the surface and molded over the centuries, the base of which was made of a rock blade that the streams had sharpened from either side; above the blade, which served as a pedestal, the rock widened to form a kind of cube, at the center of which was a hole; inside was something like a room, a small one, open on two sides parallel to the current, where part of the boulder formed the shape of a table. This rough-hewn catafalque was crowned with the vague figure of a lion.

During the month of August, this was the coolest place that existed, even when the sun was at its zenith. After some time inside, you had to cover yourself: a constant chill ran through the cave like breeze from a fan, perpetually blowing.

The bed in the rock fit all three of us at the same time. We sat on it and, refreshed from the cool air, we'd look down where the landscape opened up to the sea in the distance. It seemed to float in the sky.

It was a place of indescribable fascination that, to an untrained eye, could have appeared man-made; but anyone who knew about the architectural ability of water would have known that the stone had been carved by the river.

The place emanated magic, and we often had interesting encounters there.

Every now and then some local scholar, convinced that the past had descended from those mountains and that they had housed great civilizations, would appear with a group of other scholars whom the former had managed to persuade to visit the rock; the group would arrive full of enthusiasm and, after a quick glance at the artifact of interest, be taken in by the savage beauty of the surrounding nature and lose all interest in archaeology. Then they would take advantage of their local guide, who saw signs of ancient splendor all around them, by having him escort them around on what would become a wonderful holiday at the expense of some institution or university.

One of these expeditions surprised all three of us out of our deep slumber on the stone table. Luckily, our tent with all our gear was well camouflaged in a nearby gorge. The committee, which had come from a university in Rome, seemed pleasant enough, so we tagged along. Luciano followed behind the archaeologists, eager to impart his already vast wealth of knowledge, while Luigi and I stuck by an older, savvy geologist, whom we led around to study the local nature.

After a week Luciano had absorbed all their Roman knowledge, the geologist had gorged herself on natural wonders, and we said goodbye, all happy and satisfied with the wonderful holiday. The only disappointed one was the local scientist, whose supposedly incredible discoveries had been rejected.

My father and I had explored every corner of that land, and aside from some interesting finds from the previous century pertaining to the old brigands or World War II paraphernalia, we'd never seen anything truly ancient or immediately identifiable, though in reality there were a lot of strange things off the easily accessible trails, in places that only the shepherds knew.

Luciano told us all about his discoveries; he was a born storyteller, and when the mood struck, he would launch into a tale. Even Luigi, who was only attracted to material and practical things, would become enthralled.

Luciano always began by posing questions that he went on to answer himself: "What does your father get from goat's milk? Cheese and ricotta, same as the primordial shepherds. How many different wines did our farmers make? One red that would knock you out after one sip. What do our craftsmen do with heather? They tie the tufts together to clean pans and make little spoons with the root."

He'd provide us with examples *ad infinitum*: every type of mushroom and plant we ate, the possible uses of this or that. Then he would conclude: "We are at the dawn of history, we are in the butthole of the world and we think we're at the center, no one has ever passed through here but some lost jerk." Other times he'd conclude that our land had been inhabited by a great people who died with their swords in hand, leaving behind only those who surrendered—the worst kind of people—and we are their descendants.

I didn't wonder much about the past, but I had learned something from that unforgettable Roman geologist, who had explained to me that in antiquity, all those mountains had formed a vast and fertile plateau, inhabited by an indigenous Oscan people with subtle traces of Greek. It had been the epicenter of many great natural catastrophes—only some of which had been documented, such as the terrible earthquake of 365 BC that destroyed entire Mediterranean cities—that fractured the land, leaving it in its current state. Other floods, epidemics, and earthquakes followed in 1683, 1703, and 1908. The only certain and historically documented inhabitants were the Basilian monks, ancient missionaries of Christ who taught a little agriculture and the gospel to the vulgar pagan populations. As was plain in the etymology of our names, we were at most the progeny of bellicose and uncivilizable Oscan hunters and shepherds.

It wasn't much of an explanation for why we lived the way we did, but back then it was enough for me. My interests were directed elsewhere.

At the end of the summer leading up to our last year of school, Sante reappeared, in need of rifles, which we went about procuring in the usual way.

Every now and then the mountain would flood with hordes of barbarian destroyers: from August to November came the mushroom foragers, first for the Caesar's mushrooms and then for the black porcini of the oaks, the white ones of the pines, and the yellow ones of the holm oaks. Big vans would arrive, packed with men and women who filled plastic bags that they emptied into crates, and when they were done foraging they would stuff themselves with the food they'd brought and set off for the markets to sell their precious goods. They left all sorts of trash behind: plastic bags, empty bottles, paper. From April to July the fishermen arrived, almost never with fishing rods, but with bags of yew, cyanide tablets, hand-made bombs, and electrodes with generators. They poisoned the streams with the cyanide and the yew, which was a mortal toxin when dried and cut into thin strips. They took the biggest trout, letting the others float downstream to the sea, belly up. They placed bombs in the deepest pools of water, causing landslides; they immersed the electrodes in the smaller puddles, which immediately brought every form of life contained therein to the surface. From September to January, the hunters made their bold entrance, with filled cartridge cases that they discarded in the woods as they emptied, shooting anything that moved— including goats, cows, pigs, and sometimes even their own companions—then bragging about their exceptional bounty back in the city.

In addition to sullying the nature, this circus of characters, with the rare addition of guardians of public order and politicians, would slip off the trails and get lost in the most unexpected places, to the exasperation of those who lived in the mountains. The punishment that we normally inflicted on mushroom foragers and fishermen was to arrange it so that when they returned with the prey they had carried for miles, they would find their vehicles perched atop four pine logs.

The hunters, our favorite prey, descended from the mountain having been lightened of their rifle cartridges and wallets. When Sante made his request for rifles, we happily repeated our exploits, though on a much grander scale this time, visiting a dozen groups and hauling away more than twenty guns on our donkey's back. We'd gone too far, but it couldn't be undone.

The next morning, with the others safe in the thick of the woods, my father and I curded the cheese as we waited for the arrival of the men from the state. They presented themselves on time, but instead of the usual ironic face of Marshal Palamita, the assiduous patroller of goat pastures, we were met with the hard expressions of two of Don Peppino Zacco's soldiers.

The young thugs were arrogant in addressing my father, whom they informed that Don Peppino wanted him to know we weren't the masters of the mountain who could do whatever we pleased, that there had been important people among the hunters who'd been robbed, so we had to help the cops get the rifles back, and fast.

"Why don't you offer some ricotta to our friends, Uncle?" said Sante, appearing behind us.

The two *picciotti* grew pale, took their seats, and ate in silence.

"Tell my friend Peppino I've had a son who I named after his late friend. We're celebrating him here at my uncle's tomorrow. If he wants to honor us with his presence we'll kill a goat," Sante said, dismissing them before they'd finished their ricotta. They left without saying a word.

The next day we killed the goat, a large, meaty wether, left it to boil, and waited for the arrival of Don Peppino. In his place came a *picciotto*, hardly older than a boy, bearing his friend's apologies to Sante. By mere coincidence, that very morning the cops had served Zacco with a surveillance warrant which would prevent him from leaving the village for a couple of years. Zacco also had the *picciotto* tell us that we had done well to disarm those nosy hunters who went around without asking permission. And not only that, but he sent a necklace with two golden horns to protect the child from bad luck.

Sante sent his appreciation and gave the boy a sack containing the horns of the goat, "because my friend Peppino," he said, "is cursed by the evil eye."

Just after the boy left, the marshal of the *carabinieri*, Rosario Palamita, appeared at the sheepfold. He sat down at the table and helped himself to food, enjoying his lunch and conversing with my father about livestock and mountains. His father and his father's father had both been shepherds in Agrigento. All the while, he spoke with a wistful expression on his face.

Palamita represented the good-natured side of the state, which rarely veered out of bounds; he was prodigious with his sound advice, a good family man whose eye never wandered, but woe to anyone who exchanged conniving winks with him, lest he turn back into a *carabiniere*.

As the elders always said, "*Carabinieri* eat and drink but never sleep."

He left, grateful for lunch, and when he was a distance

away he turned back to offer Sante his best wishes for the child. Then he got into his jeep and disappeared.

"That's the second toad they'll have to swallow," my father said, worried. He wasn't referring to the police.

To cheer him up, Sante and Luciano conducted a memorable sociology lesson based on Sante's father's teachings and his experience in the field, and on Luciano's study of books and newspapers, plus his intuition and direct knowledge about some of the characters.

Their theories coincided perfectly and enriched each other.

This was more or less the story: there were only one or two true *malandrini* in each region whose identities were known to the public. Perfectly anonymous in the beginning, they became known and feared in small communities because they were subject to continuous inspections by the responsible authorities. They were often protagonists in the accounts of the local journalists, who pointed to them as possible authors of terrible crimes, and they could be seen passing through the streets of the town with their house arrest travel permits, on their way to sign themselves in on the register of individuals under surveillance. They would get arrested, but only for a few days or months, and were then banned from traveling for a time. And with all that, they suddenly found themselves enjoying the fear and consideration of everyone on a level that was out of proportion with the real danger they posed—with a criminal reputation that was induced, suggestive, constructed, in good or bad faith. These characters would go on to co-opt young men, taking care to pick the most impressionable ones.

A close look at the personal stories of the most famous *malandrini* revealed that they had ruled their small territories for decades. They enjoyed comfortable lives, spending a year or two in bed with the wives and daughters of naïve associates, another year or two in their local prisons, tended to and venerated by young recruits who, betrayed by low-lifes and informers, spent decades locked up with their lips sealed, faithful to the blood oath they'd taken with conviction. And in the end, after having lived the best possible lives permitted by their environment and abilities, and having grown too old to perform their roles and functions, they would disappear from the scene, either deliberately or not. With a bang, finished off by their successor's lead bullet, or condemned by a prosecutor intent on ensuring that evildoers spent their twilight years in jail.

It was seldom that these characters were succeeded by their own offspring, because their children grew up wearing cotton and were more inclined to become quiet and respected professionals. Acolytes were chosen from the most marginalized environments, outcasts who possessed a rebellious spirit and a need for attention. Once they had spilled their initiation blood into the circle, the unripe *picciotti* underwent a transformation, including a physical one, becoming in their speech and manner wise sixty-year-old men, and provoking the derision of savvier soldiers. They dedicated themselves entirely to serving their boss, who was an expert at life, pandering to each *picciotto*'s inclinations and abilities.

The real *malandrini* were ruthless, and although they cloaked themselves in completely amoral and falsely benevolent principles, their souls, which they had sold to the devil or whomever else, had fetched a steep price. Each one represented another opportunity to steal and exploit, even their own. Among their followers, the ones with no street smarts lost their lives or freedom, the slightly more astute retired in good order, and the wisest changed their lives and moved on.

But the godfathers certainly weren't stupid, and they knew their army was as strong as paper. When one troublemaker rebelled, the old foxes were merciless, but they showed restraint when the stray dogs were more numerous and consolidated, and instead surreptitiously plotted a tragedy, which they carried in their genetic design.

To feel secure, the bosses had to know everything. Every incident had a guilty party, not necessarily a responsible one, that was the rule, and the new affiliates had to report to the barracks before the blood from their initiation ceremony had dried on the blade that pierced their finger.

In short, the only dangerous *malandrini* were the bosses, who played with two decks of cards; they represented the anti-state while remaining at the service of someone who worked for the state. Which is why, as long as we were united, strong, and careful, we were untouchable.

One moment of weakness, real or apparent, would have destroyed us.

When Sante and Luciano had concluded this lesson, I poured another round of my famous coffee. My father went to attend to the goats in their fold, and we hid the weapons we'd taken from the hunters.

The fold was governed according to ancient rules and in Spartan style. There was a cottage, a pigsty, and a fence. The cottage was a low stone structure covered with small Roman tiles. It opened into a single room for cooking, eating, and sleeping. The ceiling height didn't exceed five and a half feet, and a few centuries earlier could have accommodated people standing upright, or almost; even modern shepherds were still as crooked as tree trunks. The single room had a hearth in a corner, the earthen floor of which was staked out with two forked poles in the ground that supported a pot for milk called a *caccamo*. On the floor there was a bed of broom, and from the support beam there hung ladles, curd breaking sticks, perforated boards and woven reed baskets for straining cheese, and all the other tools of a shepherd.

The cottage was surrounded by a fence to keep out the animals.

The pigsty was built at the bottom of a slope with beams stuck horizontally into the earth and supported at their loose ends by forked poles. The three sides that were not made of earth were closed in by dry stone walls with a single central door. Above, to cover the roof, they dumped humus from the undergrowth, which became impermeable when compressed. In front of the door stood a trough, which was filled with whey and stale bread every morning. A pig's diet was enriched with acorns and chestnuts just before slaughter; once a day it would emerge to eat and go back inside when satisfied.

The enclosure for the goats was fenced in by a succession of half-buried stakes, tied together; within the enclosure was a shelter built following the same method used for the pigsty.

The shepherds never built near a spring, their need for water being limited, as the beasts drank when grazing and their keeper with them. The goatherd never washed up; it was sufficient to wipe the inside of the crockery with whey, using tufts of heather in the winter and bunches of fern in the summer.

Shepherds hated comfort and modernity; they lived at the dawn of the world, without a care for the likes of Galileo, Leonardo, Marconi, the Savoys or the Bourbons, or even il Duce.

Against my father's resistance, we managed to modify the cottage; but my father did not let us touch the pigsty, and especially not the goat enclosure. In its former state, the cottage hadn't allowed us to stand up straight, and at night you had to decide whether to stay inside with the fleas and ticks and asphyxiate yourself with the smoke, or go out in the cold and count the stars with the goats until dawn; either misery was only bearable by continuously alternating it with the other.

Our changes were radical. We divided the room in two; we raised the walls, adapting them to the needs of the modern *homo erectus*; we covered the sleeping corner with chestnut boards and set up beds with mattresses; we opened an alcove in the wall to form a kind of bay, positioning the hearth practically outside; we outfitted it with pot racks, built a tool shed, and piped in water with a 750-yard-long rubber hose.

We renovated that place until it was almost worthy of the Middle Ages. And my father, happier than ever before, said to me, "I spent my money well sending you to school."

We also found a more permanent and practical arrangement for our weapons. Using the donkey, we began to hide them, keeping them a considerable distance from the fold. With a barbed wire fence as our reference, we started from the bottom of the hill and worked our way up the slope, digging oblong holes every hundred steps. Inside each hole we placed a plastic pipe containing a pair of firearms and their corresponding ammunition. We inserted the weapons, slathered in military grease, into inner tubes tightly bound on both sides, and then placed them inside larger pipes used for drainage. Before we buried them, we sealed the containers with rubber caps coated in hydraulic glue. This system guaranteed their perfect conservation for years to come.

Malandrini and shepherds, on the other hand, hid their weapons by wrapping them in cloth, then an endless number of plastic bags, and stashing them in hollowed tree trunks or dry stone walls, only to find the cloth was wet and the weapons rusty; they failed to realize this was the result of the small amount of air that got trapped inside the bundles, which immediately condensed onto the cloths and moistened the weapons.

For those who carried arms for reasons other than lugging around extra weight, it was essential that they were in perfect condition. As Sante always warned us, "When the time comes you can't just say, 'Hang on, let me fix this one thing.'"

We finished burying the arms at dusk. Luciano hadn't lifted a finger, as usual; he always dodged physical labor, which was tougher than he was. He was good at everything, but he had no stamina.

Luciano's stint at the Forestry Department, a public agency that hired seasonal labor to do reclamation work in the mountains, had become the stuff of legend in the region. Seven hundred thousand lire for two months. Luciano's mother, concerned about her son's apathy, and to get his nose out of his books, put him up for the job without telling him. Her son reported to work to appease her, but only for that season.

It was hard work, eight hours under the sun and 140 kilometers of travel a day, round trip. Unlucky, he found himself building dry stone walls to stop landslides, working on a team under the most feared supervisor on site, Leo Spanna, an SS sniper type, just over five feet tall, who compensated for his height by wearing a pair of tall muck boots, puffing out his chest, and walking on his toes. Everyone called him the Blowhard, and he put on airs of being a real gangster, though at his height he could have only qualified as half a gangster at most. In reality he wasn't even that; he just tyrannized everyone, held them under the whip and used the power of the pen to reduce their working hours when they needed a bathroom break.

Like all the new blood, Luciano was used as a mule. He was tasked with bringing stones for the wall from the top of the hill to the master builders at the bottom in a basket on his shoulders. He was to descend with the loads, then go back up, again and again, all day long. On his third trip it occurred to him that it might be easier to roll the stones than to carry them on his shoulders. And so he did.

This triggered a frantic flight at the bottom of the hill, and an intervention from the Blowhard; upon hearing Luciano's explanation, he began to think the boy had a screw loose. So he took pity and gave him a less strenuous task. Luciano now set off with two large buckets to be filled with drinking water for the others who were laboring under the sun. After some time passed, when their throats were parched and the

Blowhard was on the verge of exploding with unspeakable threats, the water-carrier finally appeared, holding only the handles of the buckets.

For Leo Spanna this was the proof that the student was off his rocker.

To avoid disruption at the construction site, the Blowhard, who became unexpectedly tender—defender of imbeciles that he was—brought poor Luciano into a grove of young pines that had just been planted several years before, took a small ax, and with gestures and plenty of examples, explained how to prune the trees' lower branches to make them grow faster. The supervisor departed, his heart aching, leaving his protégé to prune the pines.

At the end of the day, the Blowhard, whistling, strolled by to check Luciano's progress. His screams were so loud that everyone feared the worst. What terrible misfortune could have transpired?

The workers and supervisors came running to find Luciano laughing at the top of his lungs in a massacre of pines, all of which he had felled, and the Blowhard cussing out every saint on the calendar.

Later, after everyone had calmed down, Luciano explained that he was just fixing an ugly sight. The Blowhard didn't read between the lines at first, and approached Luciano to comfort him, at which point Luciano could no longer hold back his laughter. Then the wannabe gangster finally got the joke and blew a gasket; the only thing that saved Luciano was the ax in his hand and the intervention of the two real gangsters who had been hiding in the bushes enjoying the scene.

For months, the other supervisors would mock Spanna— the other laborers didn't dare—by shouting to him: "Do you have a good pruner you can send me?"

That was Luciano's first and only work experience, because after that his mother went to the employment office and removed him from the roster of jobseekers.

After Sante, Luigi and I had buried the weapons, we finally realized Luciano had passed the time lying on a carpet of green ferns, beaming. "Let's hope you did a good job," he said, noticing our accusatory looks. As soon as he opened his mouth, our hands automatically reached down to grab our sweaty groins, a gesture to ward off bad luck, since that wouldn't have been the first time Luciano had jinxed us with his comments.

Sante and Luciano were both good by nature, the kind of people who go through life needing the stimulus of a mission to accomplish, because otherwise they'd have succumbed to the bottle, a needle, or a speeding train. Sensitive souls with lightning minds, they each found a cause that could silence their screaming consciences: for Sante, it was dutiful vengeance in the name of his father; for Luciano, it was the pursuit of my economic prosperity, and that of my family and our wrinkle.

They were caught up in a destiny that wanted to devour them both. Sante had started to wise up, but Luciano was totally absorbed in his pursuit of my well-being. Both of them were not just the executioners but the victims of whatever they did. They were like all idealists: immersed in shit of their own making, yet somehow still candid and immaculate as lilies.

Paradoxically good and evil souls, superior minds who had followed deceptive masters because of a congenital fragility, Sante chased after his father and Luciano pursued me. They would have traveled through hell for the affection they craved, bereaved children that they were.

Those who are intrinsically good become unstoppable, like bullet trains, when they know they are right. They were like that.

Luigi wasn't. He was a cynic by nature, the runt of a sizeable litter, fighting to beat the others to the trough. His life was a race to the whey, to food, driven by an insatiable hunger. We didn't know it back then, but we were his Trojan horse. We came first in his order of affections, even above the mother who bore him, but he wouldn't have given up his food for us either. Woe to anyone who releases their hold on a bridle they once held tight.

Sante wanted to make us strong, so he invited us along on a bloody mission and we eagerly followed. We passed that last threshold of human compassion, interrupting a lively card game and leaving the two *picciotti* on the ground, taking with us the smell of gunpowder and the taste of the blood that had spattered our faces. In the distance we could hear the torment of their mothers and sisters, pursuing us down a road with no return.

After that, we saw no ghosts. None of us woke up screaming in the middle of the night. On the contrary, we passed blissfully into another dimension; we felt as if we were on a plane above everyone else, masters of their destinies. And a few months after the summer that changed everything, I repeated the experience, alone this time.

Contrary to what he'd told Don Peppino Zacco's *picciotti* who had come to demand the return of the weapons we'd stolen, Sante did not have a newborn son. In fact, his son was turning eighteen in November, and Sante had invited me to celebrate. This is how I found myself alone at the central train station in Milan. Following Sante's instructions, I took tram number thirty and got off at Porta Ticinese. Luigi had told us that in Milan people got around on these things called trams, little trains that moved on rails. It had already been decided that the following year, after graduation, we would go live there. This is also why I had gone, to get to know the city.

I found Sante's house on the Navigli and was swept up in the preparations for the party. I met his wife, a Milanese blonde who was a social worker for the city. His son, the spitting image of his mother, didn't speak Calabrese but only Italian and with a curious "r" sound that I heard for the first time.

They made me feel like family and took me shopping at Standa, at Rinascente, at Peck for goat meat. I returned home so drunk, dizzy, and loaded with gifts that it felt as if the party had been for me.

They seemed like a happy family, and I was happy with them. It was nice to eat with them, along with all their friends, including the little girlfriend of Santoro Motta, the birthday boy. Everyone tried to make sure I was comfortable.

Sante's friends were nice; they talked about legal systems, universal problems, politics. They ranted about our wasteful consumerist society, which could have saved thousands of human lives with what it was throwing out. They tried to involve me in their debates. I nodded and lowered my eyes. How removed they were from our world, I thought.

The day after my arrival, we went out alone, Sante and I, reverting to the mountaineers we'd always been, speaking dialect and back to our usual shit, which we were still unable to smell.

There were times in my life when I was full of doubt, and that's when I'd stop to observe people I met, the ones who seemed normal to me, and wish with all my heart that I could have their same thoughts, their small problems, their lives.

These moments, however, were like the shadows of passing clouds, and I'd immediately get back on my bullet train. I was fulfilling the plans I'd made for myself.

I'd gone up to Milan for several reasons.

The man who'd killed Luciano's father was Antonio Sbarra, also known as Totò the Blade, after his habit of carrying a knife everywhere, which everyone in the village knew about.

Luciano's father, a staunch socialist, former secretary of the local section of the United Socialist Party of Italy, had managed to get himself hired with the help of the party as a municipal messenger in a village close to ours. When he wasn't working, he dedicated himself to the small farm he'd received as his new wife's dowry.

And it was near that very place that his pregnant wife found him on a warm August evening, belly up, eyes to the sky, the flies and ravens already making a meal of him. He had been on the ground in a puddle of his own blood since morning.

The assassins had been particularly attentive to the poor man's nether regions, to the extent that people began to whisper that there must have been an affair. They gave the mother-to-be compassionate looks, even if everyone did their speculating behind closed doors.

During the period of public mourning, the police

were delicate, presenting themselves to search her house, informing her that she was entitled to appoint a coroner for the impending autopsy. After that, the state and the police disappeared, leaving the widow to chastely await her eternal reunion with her husband.

Some time after the fact, Totò, the man rumored to have been the executioner, moved to Turin, where he was said to have made a great deal of money on numerous kidnappings.

At my secret behest, Sante traced him.

Totò had a nice bar in the Porta Palazzo area. Sante and I passed by it a couple of times, and then he waited for me in the car. At closing time the employees said goodbye and quickly escaped the cold of winter by climbing onto packed commuter buses.

A stocky, middle-aged man lowered the shutter, calm as he could be. He lit a cigarette and walked away. He gave off an air of satisfaction. I knew a lot about him. He lived in a nice house near the bar; his sons were attending university and doing well. From his wife, a quiet woman from the South, he required no more than food on the table, obedience, and freshly-laundered clothes. And she, brought up to comply, fulfilled her husband's wishes, which she considered just. Diversions between the sheets were another matter for Totò, who procured them from a Turinese woman whom he kept in an elegant apartment on Corso Francia. A warm bed always awaited him after dinner.

Totò the Blade blissfully strolled home, taking his usual

route, believing that everyone had forgotten about the nobody he'd left on the ground with his stomach ripped open so many years before.

I walked slowly in front of him. He passed me, whistling, then stopped short: crooks can always sniff each other out. He turned around, knife in hand, and understood that it would be useless. Without altering his demeanor, he said: "Did you go to the trouble of leaving the Aurora just for me?"

"It was no trouble, I had other things to do," I replied.

"They told me you had grown, Luciano," he said.

"I'm not Luciano, but it's all the same," I said through my teeth.

He was not afraid and died with a bullet from a 357 Magnum between his eyes. The other four bullets devastated his crotch. I put my hand in my pocket, pulled out a handful of peanuts, and sprinkled them over his body.

I read the regret in his eyes: "Now, after so much effort, now that I'm no longer a pauper." His plate and bed were growing cold. Totò would be late that evening.

I left him there, a son of the Aspromonte, to stain the sidewalks of the North.

They called us the "children of the forest," we descendants of the people who had inhabited the woods of the Calabrian massif for millennia, we who'd transformed it into a place of evil, we who'd given up the Aspromonte to conquer another world.

———

"Our kidnapping work is about to end," Sante told me after we were back in Milan.

The state could no longer bear the idea of its rich taxpayers visiting our mountains and fattening up the *malandrini* and shepherds on their ransoms. Instead, the state was offering the children of the Aspromonte new and easier ways to make money. Soon, all the shepherds' children would move to the North to sell drugs. Our fathers had driven away an entire generation of entrepreneurs, economic pioneers who might have effected a shift in the country, urbanizing masses of peasants, generating prosperity and modernity, and allowing us to glimpse a different future. The fruit of their labor had been yielding a more liberated population of former ditch-diggers and budding proletarians.

Those northern entrepreneurs, however, overestimated themselves, and we, the presumed beneficiaries of their economic revolution, who were much more determined and focused, forced them under their own yoke, imprisoned them in the mountains, and took them for all they were worth.

"Our fathers stopped them," Sante said. "We're going to use their own money to burn down their children's future . . . And ours, too."

Sante stopped talking and showed me the work he'd been doing lately.

He counted out six million lire on the kitchen table, put it in a paper bag, and we left. At the bar we drank a coffee—sludge compared to the coffee I made in the mountains, he admitted. Sante waited for a table to free up and went to sit with a Sicilian, exchanged a few words, left the bag, and walked away with an envelope. We took the tram and went into another bar. Sante sat down, I drank another coffee, and we left with a different envelope. Then, at his house, on the kitchen table, he counted out nine million lire. These were the Milanese heists that the Calabrians were about to monopolize, he explained, adding that "the Slavs and the blacks bring in women to comfort the same guys from Milan we used to imprison in the mountains; except now, with the help of the Turks, we deal them brown sugar instead," he said.

After that lesson, we devoted ourselves to one of the other reasons I'd come to Milan. He drove me out of town, toward the paddy fields near Pavia, and I felt lost. How could they live on that endless plain? How did they know where they were going? Without even a bump in the ground to anchor our view, or a single point of reference, we traveled for hours through frost-covered fields interrupted by rows of perfectly spaced poplars. What strange beings lived here? They could have been raising millions of beasts on their land—not goats, which would immediately flee to a higher altitude, but stupid and productive sheep. Instead they devastated the landscape with smoky factories.

I remembered the stories of our elders, who had begun

to refer to all northerners as Piedmontese after Garibaldi came through, back when they still occupied the mountains. They repeated the stories of their grandparents, who swore they saw the giant Piedmontese making a game of tossing around the granite stones from the village mills—stones that weighed half a ton.

I scanned the gates of the many farmhouses dotting the plains, fearing I might see a Piedmontese giant emerge from one.

We passed through places whose names randomly imprinted on my mind as they appeared on the road signs. La Certosa di Pavia, Zeccone, Stradella, San Martino, Siziano, Bascapè, Vellezzo Bellini. One day, I'd learn to love those plains, which emanated a sad sweetness on foggy days like no other place in the world.

We conducted the necessary visits and a few days later we left in the car. Kidnapping season was coming to an end, as Sante said, and we were going to close it with a job all our own.

Heading south toward Calabria, I came to know our country in its entire expanse for the first time looking out the window of a car.

THE BOYS
OF THE
AURORA

When we entered the Aurora on our way home from Milan, no one came out to greet us. As I stepped through the door of my house, loaded with presents, my five sisters, the little queens, didn't jump all over me like they usually did when I brought packages for them.

There had been two funerals in the village during the same week I had been away.

Totò the Blade's cronies had brought him home, after all those years; he arrived in a luxurious walnut box, in a shiny hearse that drove him to a monumental funeral chapel of white marble, a testament to the fortune he'd made.

And Luciano's mother had been buried too, carried on the shoulders of neighbors from the Aurora, followed by almost everyone from the rest of the village. But she, unlike Totò, had found a place in the bare earth, next to her husband.

Poor woman. Confined to widowhood in black for almost twenty years, she seemed to have been blossoming again in recent days, shedding her drab attire in favor of more youthful clothes that made her look as vibrant as a virgin just before her wedding day. And now she was dead.

According to tradition, the mourning period continued for eight days after the funeral to allow everyone to participate in the grieving, to keep the next of kin company and alleviate their suffering. No matter who had died, for the entire eight days every television or radio in the village would be switched off; meanwhile, close relatives of the deceased deprived themselves of such entertainment for the whole of the first year. The houses with black rags hanging from their doors became meeting places for the villagers, and as often happens, the tragedy transformed into a farce. Mourning became a party. Visitors were required to bring food to fortify the mourners, and a competition ensued over who brought the most and the best. There was a constant stream of trays of milk, coffee, and pastries of every kind, which comforted those who came to visit and reminisce about the departed's best qualities. We spent entire days sharing fond memories and funny stories, the perfect setting for anyone who needed to be filled in on the events of the last fifty years, and there was always more laughter than tears. A lost woodsman would have thought he had stumbled upon a wedding banquet rather than a funeral.

After three days of bacchanalia, Luciano was unable to bear any more, and shut out his mother's admirers, who he hadn't known were so numerous. He was alone in his mourning and alone in the world.

For the Christmas holidays, Anna came down to see Sante and brought a couple from Milan with her. They stayed in Luciano's empty house.

We spent Christmas according to tradition, in the mountains for the slaughter of the pig—a celebration within a celebration. Two days of incredible food and drink—back then, not even the women were concerned with dieting or cholesterol.

On the first day we killed the beast, laid it out on a bench, and skinned it with boiling water. As it hung upside down, we gutted and quartered it, selecting cuts for capicolli, bacon, ribs and salted lard. Then we deboned the meat for sausages and soppressata.

Once the meat was divided, it was given to the women to be cleaned of waste. They also washed out the intestines, which would be used for the sausage casings, and then left everything to rest for twenty-four hours.

Having finished our duties, we men gathered by the hearth and took turns recounting our incredible adventures over the continuous clink of glasses, slices of goat's cheese, and hunks of fatty roasted meat.

What a spectacle, my mother orchestrating the women in their chaotic work, the Calabrian-Milanese group comprising

Sante's guests, my sisters, and a couple of girls from the Aurora who had come up the mountain to help us and have a good time. Miraculously, between all the gossip and laughter that persisted late into the evening, they managed to complete their tasks.

The following day, when the meat had been dried to perfection, the women stuffed the sausages, wrapped the capicolli, rolled up the bacon, and salted and peppered the ribs and the lard, which were hung from the rafters to age in the smoke and the cold for at least twenty-five days. The remaining meat filled an entire pot, and in the late evening, after it had been cooking on oak embers for eight hours, it was ready to be eaten. The wine began to flow, and with clinking glasses and rhyming poetry we greeted the sunrise.

The guests were thrilled. They'd never imagined that the people from the Aspromonte could be such fun. We were surprised in turn—what strange people, the Milanese, encountering everything with a childlike spirit, without reservations or prejudices.

After their work was done, the women returned to the village to bake cakes for the feast of San Silvestro, while the men continued their party on the mountain. Even Anna's friend refused to be torn away. The group was also joined by one of my father's elderly cousins, Beniamino, to whom God had not granted children. He lived in the Aurora, and having recently been widowed, he had become part of our family, like an old grandfather. Bino, as everyone called him, was the historian of those mountains, the greatest connoisseur of goats and brigands. If you put a kid goat in front of him he could guess its parents without fail: "They're like people, and the children always look like their parents," he said. He called the beasts by ancient names according to their colors, the patterns of their coats, and their physical characteristics.

He'd been a gangster as a young man and had tried his luck in America. He'd had some kind of racket going for a few years in Broccolino and, after a stint in jail, was kicked out of town. Back in the village he married, retired in good order, and dedicated himself to the goats. After his third glass of wine, he would always interject an English "Dat's awright" and recount his American adventures. His best one was a true story about Joe Petrosino. He claimed to have met all the big shots in person in America, including the hit men hired by Vito Cascieferru—as he called him, mangling Don Vito's name—to kill the gangster. The most dangerous of the crew were two of our own boys from Savignana, a nearby village. Bino claimed that the two *picciotti*, under the pretext of returning to Italy to see their families, went all the way to Palermo to make the hit. "One of them died here and I was the one to offer condolences to their next of kin," he said. At that point we'd tell him he was full of it, and Bino, invoking the Madonna of the Mountain, said, "I can say it now, no one here knew them, and in any case they're dead now and the bill was never paid." And then he'd say, "Their names were Tano Misiti and Rocco Tripepi. Just say the word and I'll take you to Savignana. Tripepi's granddaughter is alive and well and has photos of her *nonno* with Cascieferru."

Then he'd continue his story: "In the fifties, the Malupassu caves were the refuge of wanted men, known in those days as brigands. One year there were fifty-six of them, all from the surrounding villages. No one, cop or otherwise, could get anywhere near the caves, since the brigands were armed. I was the only one who managed to climb to the top of the mountain and feast with them. They had a party up there every day. And every night, the brigands would take turns going down to the sea in small raiding groups to capture animals and men. Their enclosures were always full of beasts to be either resold or eaten, and there were always hostages in the caves, rich landowners or noblemen. During the flood of '51 that devastated half of the Aspromonte villages and forced us to abandon the mountain for the putrid swamp where we live now, the brigands preyed on so many people that the state, perturbed by their fame, sent a large army to disperse them. They didn't manage to capture a single one, and when the brigands all scattered there was no pasture or house in the Aspromonte that didn't welcome them. The Military Engineers mined most of the caves and ended the party at Malupassu."

It was true that in the place Bino named, inside caves hidden by vegetation, it was not uncommon to find cowhides with old guns and other objects sewn inside of them.

But the story I liked most was the one about the wolf, and if there were willing hands to pour wine and stoke the fire, Bino would go on without a break.

"Ancient goatherds loved the wolf and considered it a faithful companion and friend, unlike modern shepherds, who see it as a ravenous predator and persecute it with shotguns, traps, and poison—and selfishly so, because to save a few heads they make the entire herd suffer. The ancient shepherd didn't consider himself the exclusive owner of the flock, knowing he had an invisible partner in the wolf. Only in modern times do domestic dogs have a place in an Aspromonte fold; it didn't used to be that way. Contrary to common belief, the Calabrian wolf didn't hunt in a pack. It was a skittish and solitary animal that sought out others of its kind only to howl and reproduce. Each animal would choose a pasture, a shepherd, a flock, and become a part of it. It would follow the flock to pasture and scare off the foxes and the eagles that would descend after their prolonged acrobatics to go after the newborns; they would chase off the boars and devour their offspring, who destroyed the pastures. Every now and then the wolf would satiate its hunger for days by picking off a single goat. It waited for the beasts to graze and chose only one, taking care to always target the oldest and feeblest, contributing to genetic selection by ensuring that the best beasts survived. The lost beasts were soon replaced by newborns. Back before the days of veterinarians it was rare to see such splendid herds outside of the Aspromonte. Today's shepherd wants to keep everything for himself, and so the old and sick beasts end up at the butcher's and in the stomachs of duped customers. The persecuted wolves are forced to hunt in packs and visit all the folds, and if they manage to penetrate one or find an unguarded herd, the shepherd finds himself without a flock, having lost a thousand sheep to save twenty. The elders say that when there was still a king in Naples, a pious goatherd found shelter for his goats inside an old hunting lodge, instead of the typical enclosure. As usual, on Christmas Eve, he fulfilled his vow to the Madonna of the Mountain and returned to the village to attend the celebration of the birth of baby Jesus. After herding the beasts into the shelter and closing them in, he set out under a starry sky to witness the sacred mystery. The joyous event was marked by a sudden, dense snowfall that made the replica saint look almost like the real thing. By dawn, the blanket of snow had reached disproportionate heights, the creeks were spilling over, and the pious herdsman was trapped in the village for that day, then the next, and every day after that until the feast of San Silvestro. If they had been in their enclosure, the goats could have climbed over the snow to hop the fence and find something to eat, even if it had only been the tops of trees. But they were trapped in the lodge. When death was near and the beasts were gnashing at each other's coats, mournfully bleating, a wolf dug a tunnel, first through the snow and then between the door and the earth, and led the herd out of their mortal trap in single file. The pious goatherd, having risked his life to get back to his herd, found the goats grazing peacefully on the tops of the holm oaks as if they were low-lying bushes. From that day forth the goats would only enter the hunting lodge if he pulled them in by force, and while the goatherd certainly never saw the wolf, he did see the tunnel and all the paw prints encircling the lodge, as if every wolf on the mountain had gathered there."

Sante and Anna's friend was a city councilman and well-known professional in Milan—a liberal socialist of the old guard, not one of those bigoted moralists. Of course we never had any suspect conversations, we never showed our weapons, but he certainly wasn't stupid and must have noticed that we weren't making enough cheese to sustain our standard of living which, if not luxurious, was dignified enough. He had a free spirit and enjoyed the holiday to its fullest. By now, he explained, Calabrians made up a substantial part of the Milanese electorate and a healthy curiosity had prompted him to get to know his constituents. We took him to explore the mountain, with Luciano pegged to his side, happy to have found a sponge like himself who was onto the next question before you could answer the first.

Nothing escaped the man, like how we placed one stone atop a heap of stones in our path. The third time he saw us do this, he stopped us and asked. The repetition of the gesture, deprived of such an explanation, made the man wonder if it was conditioned, a product of habit devoid of rationale. He insisted that Luciano explain its meaning, if it had one.

It was not a conditioned gesture: each change in the mountain slope was marked with an ordered mound of stones. The pagans used to add a stone to the top of the heap as a gift, to appease the spirits of the woods and secure protection for the traveler. The size of the mound indicated the number of devotees who had passed through. From the moss that had accumulated on a pile, which was topped by a few clean stones, it was clear that this form of worship was limited to a few stubborn followers. Despite being covered in moss, the pagan simulacra on that path had a particular value—based on the size of the heap of stones, they were watching over the oldest paths on the whole mountain. We were retracing the steps of the Saint, the protector, along with the pagan gods of the shepherds, and of those lands. In our worship we allowed no room for irony; we were as observant as our early predecessors.

When the Basilian monks arrived around the year one thousand, the mountain populations were succumbing to the miseries and diseases that had decimated the natives. The last of the mountain people didn't have the strength to repel the strangers as they had done for centuries, and surrendered to the army of God, who gave them the means of their survival. This particular order, the Basilians, were made up of literate peasants; they constructed churches and introduced agriculture, transforming shepherds into tillers of the soil. All the monks were saints. But the agricultural science at the time could not overcome all the challenges, and crops refused to grow in the highest mountains where the toughest shepherds lived. The Saint left his brothers to their ministries in the lower mountains and ascended to save our ancestors from the path we were treading. Crossing the pass to the highest mountain, he worked for months. Armed with an ax, he skinned pines and extracted the pitch, which he molded into balls, and then placed the balls on the bare rocks. He went on this way, unflagging. From the forest, our forebears fearfully watched the stranger, believing him to be an evil spirit that had come to destroy their woods. But the man's meekness gradually prevailed over their mistrust and fear. The Saint became familiar to the shepherds, who would approach him in groups. The pine pitch balls transformed to bread, and all the shepherds fed on it. To thank the Saint, the people of the forest sacrificed their biggest fir tree and made him a wooden throne so his tired limbs could rest. When, after countless years of hard dedication to the poor, the Saint returned to his Heavenly General, the shepherds placed him in a pine coffin and walked in reverse along the path the monk had taken to reach them. They walked for miles, and when the fatigue overpowered them, they stopped. In that spot, they buried the Saint and built his church. At each crossroads on the path created by their benefactor, the shepherds would build their pagan heaps to enshrine the fusion of two worlds, the old and the older. In those who still honor the ancients, that union lives on.

After Luciano's explanation, we continued on the path, passing more heaps. We kept climbing. With the last summit in view, we crossed a river over a footbridge of bound logs. On the other side, at the foot of the summit, we came across a huge log on the ground that looked like a wooden seat.

The man's legs began to tremble.

We urged him onward, to the top of the mountain, where I pointed to a spot straight ahead of us, miles away in the foothills where the Saint's church rose up, and placed the binoculars in his hands.

He was overcome, his knees buckled, and only his socialist atheism kept him from crossing himself. To reassure him, each one of us, even Sante, took out the goatskin pouch we carried everywhere. Each contained a little picture depicting the Saint with the ax in one hand and a ball of pitch in the other, all tolerated by the Holy Mother Church which, though it had never officially canonized the man, had never quashed his following. This was the nature of the Aspromonte: even the holiest things were profane, the most beautiful flower possessed a thorn, and the most righteous man a rifle hidden somewhere in the woods.

In addition to the little pictures, our pouches contained a

precise number of pebbles, depending on the meaning that each person assigned to the number, picked from the debris that formed at the foot of the pagan altars.

Saints and the spirits of the woods, equally sacred, were one and the same, and we wouldn't have traveled a step without them to guard our path.

We celebrated the New Year together. The first of January was a memorable day. The Milanese got tanned—drunks were known as "tanners" in our parts—and by late evening, when it was time for him to go, he had to steady himself to say his goodbye. We all hugged, and old Bino almost cried; the councilman left handfuls of business cards, making it known that he was "at the disposal of our friends."

After a few days being our guests, they went down to the village to stay at Luciano's house. The Aurora, our wrinkle, was our kingdom, as much so as the part of the mountain where my father grazed his flock.

After the flood in the fifties, our village had been rebuilt several miles from the old mountain home, halfway between the sea and the foothills, in a fetid swamp that they called the malaria fields. The people of the forest had been moved from the peaks of the Aspromonte all the way down to the sea because of floods, real or presumed. Dozens of yellowish barracks had sprung up on an area of half a square mile to welcome the mountain refugees. The new town wasn't even a town but an enclave in the territory of another municipality, far from the mountains that our people had populated for millennia, and far from everything we had called our own. We were a confused populace who could no longer hunt or graze our flocks, and who would perhaps never learn to fish.

Outside of the village, my friends and I represented all the children of the forest; among the villagers, Luigi, Luciano, and I were distinguished by the wrinkle we lived in, the Aurora. The wrinkle was a rectangle of road across which two buildings faced each other, eight apartments on two floors on one side and the same on the other. To the people in the village, the three of us were known as the boys of the Aurora.

When the Milanese left, Luigi, Luciano, and I stayed in the mountains for another week on our own, under Bino's watch.

We missed our new friends, and tried to distract ourselves.

I happened to notice very fresh cow tracks in the part of the pasture that my father reserved for the harshest period of winter. The cows were feral, wandering free without masters, in groups of ten or twenty, accompanied by a single bull. They were small, native beasts, their color ranging from gray to black. They lived quietly, undisturbed, and always kept their distance from people. When someone got too close, they would burst into a wild gallop whose echo would fill the mountain. Minutes later, they could be seen peacefully grazing on a distant ridge.

Their minute size allowed them to adapt to their unforgiving habitat. Heftier beasts would have ended up at the bottom of a ravine, or dead from starvation. The type of grazing offered by the Aspromonte wouldn't have been enough to fill the stomachs of larger cows.

I'd always perceived the fear and reverence that the villagers felt toward the cows, but the explanations I'd heard for their presence were muddled and contorted. I came to the bold conclusion that we hid behind our myths about the cows because we'd been so unsuccessful at hunting them.

I had sometimes observed the herds from afar with binoculars. The beasts walked like a small army, with one of the two oldest cows at the head of the herd and the other at the tail. When they came out of the woods to graze in an open space, the leader would arrive first, crossing the entire pasture, sniffing at the air, and only when she lowered her head to graze all the others would emerge. After a time the rearguard would join them.

The cows grazed in a circle, inside of which the calves played. At the exact center of the formation was the sire.

The two elder cows always remained at a distance; it was hard to get them within firing range, and even if that were possible, their old meat would have only been good for boiling. Their society was matriarchal, directed by the females in order of age. They chose the bull from among the best males and chased away their other sons.

When we found the cow prints in my father's pasture, Bino tried to dissuade me from going after them. I didn't listen.

I grabbed the rifle, loaded the cartridge, and at dawn I squatted at the edge of the clearing and waited for the cows to come graze. My limbs were already numb from the cold and from holding my position when the sentry finally made her entrance. She spread her nostrils and blew hard. She looked in every direction, including mine, but did not see me. Then she quietly lowered her head to plunder the grass that belonged to my goats. A moment later, from the woods, the playful group emerged.

The females of this herd had outdone themselves. As I had already observed from my binoculars, they had raised themselves a huge sire, twice their size, with a short, silky coat, black and shining. It was feminine greed that led to the bull's demise. Their protective circle proved to be a useless defense. No matter how small the beast made itself, its head and shoulders still rose above the circular trench of horns.

The shot was sudden. The thunderous bang had the effect of a stone in a placid pond. The circle drifted, the animals carried away in waves. The bull seemed surprised, as if he had been caught naked. For an eternal instant, he stood frozen.

Alone. In the middle of the deserted clearing.

I found myself on my feet without realizing I had moved. Target detected.

I had been sure I'd hit the bull, but the opposite seemed true.

I waited, lucid and stiff, for death to take me, my chest ready to embrace the blow.

The bull came to a halt ten yards away from me. I could read his thoughts for a moment. He had a gruesome hole between his eyes, from which an incredible stream of blood and yellow matter emerged. His eyes were pointed toward me but not looking at me. They were staring at something or someone not of this world.

The animal had already been dead a few seconds. He just didn't know it, or didn't want to believe it.

A vaporous rush of urine sprayed from his huge penis, signaling the release of his muscles, his loss of control. He collapsed.

Soon Luciano and Luigi arrived with their large military backpacks. They knew I'd never missed a shot as a hunter. This time, however, there wasn't the usual lighthearted scene with our constant jokes. We quartered the beast, selecting only the best cuts. We took as much meat as we could carry.

We found the heavy Brenneke slug inside its ribcage. It had devastated the mighty animal, traveling three feet inside its body, through its head and neck, and down into its white lungs.

We carried the heavy load to the fold. It was a dull day.

We tended to the goats in silence and retired early without eating.

That night was harrowing. I thought I could hear a mournful bellowing. I saw the bull's head staring at me with that terrible, dripping, artificial eye in the middle of his forehead. Suddenly the image changed and the bull took on the appearance of Totò the Blade. An immense pain overtook me, I was aware I was trapped in a nightmare. I tried to wake up and couldn't, I got up and fell back down, and only when the pain had traveled to my core could I shake myself awake.

I found myself sitting up in the dark. Bino tenderly pressed a cup of hot coffee into my hands. "Did you hear them?"

I looked at him, dumbfounded.

"No, they weren't in your head, they always do that when they lose a friend. They walk in circles all night around the body and let out frightful moans. Sometimes they go on like that for months, some even let themselves die. The ancients said the cows belong to the spirits of the woods. I've never experienced it myself, but I've seen shepherds as proud as you wake up in the morning destroyed and watch the darkness fall with terror. We are a part of the mountains, not their masters. Sometimes practicing evil is necessary to survive. Taking a life is always wrong. But if you don't give your conscience an alibi or a decoy, it will scream at you every night. Come, we have to appease them."

We went out into the night. We laid the meat on the piles of stones along the path of the Saint.

My young mind soon muffled my throbbing heart, and the episode went off to languish in a dark corner of my psyche.

When we returned to the village, our friends had already left for Milan. We would encounter the councilman again in Milan, before he plunged into the abyss.

Sante had advised my father to get ready for spring. One last job, a kidnapping of our own.

Before he left, the councilman had met with some party friends in the city and extended a precious gift to my father and others in the wrinkle: a hiring letter from the Forestry Agency, offering a permanent, long-term contract. It meant a fixed salary, however modest. Something my father could have only dreamed of. That money, even if it came late—too late for me—restored my father's dignity and his role as head of the household.

The most incredible thing to him was his job title. They had hired him as a forest ranger. So now they were paying him to do what he had always done for free, as a natural call of duty: defend his mountain.

Luciano, Luigi, and I devoted ourselves almost exclusively to our books. That year was fundamental for us; we had to prepare for graduation and we did so with purpose, like everything else we did. We had good teachers, capable people who helped everyone, especially us, the children of the forest. They never wrote us up, never called our parents. They simply shared their love of books and culture. They had taught us how to be with others and feel included. In the end, we didn't become who we had because of them, or because society was dirty, ugly, and bad. There were very few dirty, ugly, and bad men. But their culture was dominant. And the misery was oppressive. There was no door in the Locride, our patch of Reggio Calabria, that hadn't seen the boots of the military police on its threshold; the *carabinieri* were the only faces of the state we knew in our part of the world.

The only person of good repute that the Locride had produced in decades was Corrado Alvaro. Either the inhabitants were genetically predisposed to crime or there was an interest, historically perpetuated, in the reproduction of generations of criminals.

If mountain boys like us had strayed from our roots, perhaps it was because we had been forced to choose between a life of service or our own demise—unless we chose self-defense.

We had chosen to live freely but armed, ready to defend or attack, whether our enemies were gangsters or cops.

Our money was running out. Luciano's only inheritance from his mother had been a funeral to pay for. He'd lent me some money, and I repaid what little I could. He had never kept his share from our raids for himself. Everything we collected we divided into three, and most of his share would invariably end up spent on members of my family and others in the Aurora.

It's still a mystery how Luigi managed to burn through his cash without leaving anything at home or offering charity around the Aurora aside from a few coins here and there. The fact is that every time we divided our funds, he would appear shortly thereafter to beg for more.

So Luciano and I, in the black, would apply ourselves to our books, and Luigi would sneak off to find money, which had become his specialty. He had a nose for opportunity like he had for beautiful women, and sometimes he combined the two. When he told us about an idea for a hit, we were fascinated by his vision.

He had been working on it in secret for four years, he confided to us. The thought had come to him the night we became men. While Luciano and I, red in the face, confronted the memorable and frightful undertaking, he was already running the numbers.

The Valenciano hotel—who would have ever dreamed it up?

We had gone about twice a month over the last few years just to fuck. But Luigi had been working overtime. In addition to making love, he secretly met up with some of the girls to work on the hit, or just passed by the Valenciano to see what was going on. He was sure now that his plan was ready.

We all knew the Valenciano's owner and pimp, Vittorio

Patti, a fat Sicilian pig. We almost always saw him at the hotel. Luigi had learned everything else we'd need to know.

The pimp had a permanent cohort of five or six girls, most of them foreign. The girls spent a few months satisfying Calabrian cravings, then disappeared overnight, only to be replaced by new ones. Professionals in the trade knew that fresh goods were necessary to fuel desire.

Vittorio Patti had an associate in Milan who sent him girls. Before he parted with the new merchandise, however, the said associate wanted his half of the earnings, and the pimp, as trusting as a convict before his executioner, would deliver it to him personally. Now and then, he would suddenly disappear from circulation along with the booty.

Calculating that the girls brought in at least two million a day—or sixty million a month—minus twenty percent, deducting for the ladies' room and board, minus the ten percent kickback the Blood Brothers took, the pimp's purse must have contained anywhere from sixty to one hundred million lire on his periodic travels to Milan.

Where he kept the money, when and how he traveled, and with what or whom remained a mystery for years.

Vittorio Patti, besides all his other sins, which were many, was a known sex fiend, and every night the women would work overtime for him, stopping by his house in shifts. Many times the fat Sicilian had seemed to be on the verge of giving up his secrets to the girls Luigi had engaged, but he would always manage to exhaust his desires a moment before making the fatal disclosure.

Things continued this way until Natalia, the gypsy from Andalusia, appeared at the Valenciano. It wasn't because of her looks, which were rather average, that the pig sang for her, but because she was guardian of many secrets pertaining to the art of love.

Luigi had the chance to be one of the very first customers to enjoy her esoterics. The gypsy immediately signed on to his plan. To the great disappointment of the many enthusiasts who were eager to reconfirm the Andalusian woman's talents, she grew stingy in distributing her pleasures, including to her pimp.

When she was convinced that he had been baited long enough, Natalia dusted off her skills and left Patti so stunned that he asked her to move in with him. He had never known such a mantis, as he would confide in anyone.

Like the time we robbed the post office, Luigi appeared at my house in the middle of the night to announce that the moment had arrived. Even in his cooked state, the pimp had been cautious enough not to tell Natalia of his departure until the last minute, so she barely had time to prepare the suitcases. They would be traveling together, doves on their honeymoon, in a sleeper cabin on the 1 A.M. Syracuse-Milan express train.

We didn't require bags, so we jumped in the car and got ourselves onto the fast train, having discreetly boarded one stop after the couple.

In order not to raise suspicions about the sly Spaniard, we needed to make our hit as far as possible from the city.

Natalia and Luigi had agreed on a signal. When, a few minutes before we arrived in Naples, the Spaniard opened the door for us, we found the maniac in such a state of bliss that he didn't even hear the wood cracking between his head and neck. His faithful concubine defended the luggage tooth and nail, and could only be overpowered by a direct hit that left an evident bruise.

We got off the train quietly and left the suitcases in the baggage deposit, happily ducking into the alleyways of the kingdom's ancient capital.

By the time the lovebirds came to, they were well on their way to Rome.

Why would Patti report the heist? To be ridiculed for the rest of his days? In Naples even the clumsiest villains carried a knife to fend off the inevitable thieves. Rather, he had been lucky to have gotten away with his carelessness so many times before. From then on he would always travel accompanied by two *picciotti*.

With what money his wise Spanish companion had hidden in her intimate regions—the only part of the cabin that hadn't been plundered by the voracious thieves—they visited Rome. Patti consoled his lover with an unusual tenderness and, after an unforgettable night in a hotel, they traveled back to the toe of the boot.

When they got back to the Valenciano, Natalia gradually returned to her ordinary intimate duties and, a few months later, Patti sent her back to Milan without much of a thought. There, she was her own boss, and secured a dignified salary for herself with the help of her crotch. With the fat man's money and her savings, she invested in a business that would become a place of leisure for the stressed go-getter Milanese.

We would meet again.

After the robbery we explored the length and breadth of Naples, from the monstrous suburbs to the elegant salons in the city center, and in the evening we collected the luggage in anticipation of a pleasant return journey, which it was.

We took seats in a compartment already occupied by a young, off-duty auxiliary *carabiniere* who got off at Paola, and an elderly couple who were returning to Catanzaro after visiting their children in the North.

We told them we were headed to the extreme south of the peninsula, not specifying the location, and claimed we were exhausted after having endured the difficult entry tests for government jobs. We conversed cheerfully, as was customary on the rancid carriages of the oil trains.

The retired old man, who had served the state as a clerk

at the capital's Tribunal for forty years, held court. He had
known misfortunes and recounted many.

After a few hours of conversation, when confidence had
loosened the grip of our ironclad Calabrian discretion, the
former quasi-magistrate asked us the name of our town.
Before we could stop him, Luigi blurted it out.

The old man choked on a gasp. "The Salters!" he cried.
He grabbed his terrified companion and dragged her and
their suitcases to another carriage, leaving us all with our
mouths agape, including the cop.

We knew the history of the salters well. Our grandparents had been known by that name in the forties. The
incident had happened just before the new Caesar dragged
us into the second war, back when the village was still high
in the mountains.

A group of hungry thieves from the countryside had
raided animals that were the property of a wealthy doctor
in Lica, a nearby village, then hid away the animals in
the less accessible mountain pastures. Every so often they
invited groups of friends to gorge themselves on the stolen
loot. One of the occasional guests, a certain Peppe Tavilla,
had been spotted on the road to Lica, where the beasts had
grazed peacefully before they had been spirited up to the
mountains.

The poor man, in fact, was on his way to meet with a
lawyer; Lica was the county seat of the magistrate's court,
and the nearest place to find one. He had been made the

beneficiary of a small inheritance from a late relative who had emigrated to America, and given the misery of those days, he met with the expert jurist three times, fearfully and covertly, to sort out the necessary paperwork.

A hateful gossipmonger, a childless woman—a *zire,* as they called women who couldn't reproduce—used the time on her hands to keep abundant watch over her neighbors. The snake lived in a miserable hovel that faced the road connecting the two villages, and had thrice seen a wary Peppe Tavilla plodding toward Lica.

She insinuated that Tavilla was a snitch, and the idea soon took root in other minds darkened by misery and ignorance.

When he received an invitation to another feast, the man's eyes brightened in anticipation, given his memory of the previous ones; his meager legacy had certainly not made him a wealthy man.

Because guests usually made a contribution, Peppe asked the man bearing the invitation what he could bring. "We're running low on salt in the mountains," the latter replied.

Peppe happily set off for the feast with a bag full of salt. But instead of a banquet, he found himself faced with seven sharp blades that carved him up alive. The thieves sprinkled salt on his freshly opened wounds to heighten his agony.

Poor Peppe. A victim, like so many others, of a dissatisfied whore.

The victims also included the seven murderers, who paid

for their crime with decades of hard jail time, following a trial that revealed their victim's innocence.

The trial generated so much uproar that to avoid unrest and lynching attempts they decided to move it from the criminal court of Calabria to the Tribunal of Catanzaro. Wherever people from my village went, they were denied even a glass of water if they revealed their origins: "The Salters, God forbid!"

One of the seven Salters was still alive and could be found sitting out on the benches of the square in the middle of our new village.

After the clerk ran off, our conversation died and we resigned ourselves to sleeping until we arrived in the city. We got off the train and boarded a bus that brought us back to the village. Back in the hollow, we slipped into Minna Bonasira's house, opened Patti's bag, and discovered that the mighty Calabrian gonads had gifted us with sixty-three million lire, in addition to Natalia's share of twenty-one million. Minna slipped the cash we gave her between her breasts and took her rugrats shopping in the village. We hid the bag full of money in the armoire in Minna's bedroom under lock and key and went back home to wash up. A few hours later, we reconvened and celebrated with Minna late into the night.

Minna's home was our lair in the Aurora. Her real name

was Mina, the diminutive of Girolama, but the mountains that protruded from her chest had earned her the additional "n," which spelled out "breast" in our Calabrese dialect, and she had accepted the name from everyone in the hollow without protest.

Minna was not from the village, but she appeared one day and occupied a house abandoned by a family that had gone off in search of fortune. She had come to the hollow with an engineer who worked for a company that ran phone cables along the coast. Scarcely more than a girl, she arrived in the village with her belly already swollen, and by the time the engineer disappeared when the company contract finished just a year later, Minna's belly had grown again. Nobody in the hollow ever asked about her private life. They accepted her, and she remained with her two tots. She got by taking little jobs in the fields or in the homes of the wealthy, finding acceptance in the Aurora. When the city brothels lost their luster, we took our turns in her bed, starting with Luigi. And her house became a refuge for our weapons and plunder.

After our train hit, we waited quietly for spring to arrive, and cut back on our visits to the Valenciano. We didn't miss any more school, we were good students, and spring took us by surprise one Sunday in the woods.

To announce it were the amorous effusions from the

jaybirds, treacherous mountain spies. A gossipy bunch, perennially alert and inevitably the first to notice anything, they notified one another of every human or animal presence with their croaking.

The impetuous streams had quieted, and we were ready. At the end of March, Sante loaded us into his car and we presented ourselves at an appointment we hadn't been invited to.

The flatlands of northern Italy were still immersed in winter, and a thick fog accompanied us into the Po Valley countryside. Behind a beautiful, recently-restored farmhouse, the dogs, naive as their masters, licked our gun-gripping hands, and escorted us tranquilly to an illuminated set of French doors.

One kick was enough to break them in. Minutes later, we had gathered the quiet little family in the living room, including the nanny, since the northerners employed foreigners to raise their children. The mother cooperated and helped to calm her two splendid teenage daughters.

Despite the monstrosity of what we were doing, we still had some principles left, and instead of going for this easy prey we patiently waited for the head of the household to arrive.

He came up the stairs from the garage. He was a handsome man, about fifty, tall and slim, sporting a suit and tie. He wore a gold watch on his wrist and a Tincati cashmere coat. He was a hot-shot manager in Milan who had been among the first to prosper before the city entered its roaring '80s.

He calmly registered the situation. He made sure everyone was okay, hugged his daughters, dispensed a series of recommendations, and left with us almost as if he had a business appointment that required his presence elsewhere. The most important thing for him was to keep them safe. He let us handcuff him and waited as we locked up his girls, perfectly unharmed, in the bathroom on the second floor. Relieved, he allowed himself to be blindfolded and, with his eyes and ears covered, he was transported away from his kingdom prostrate in the backseat of our car, by four foreigners who had arrived from another world.

Thirty minutes later, the car slid into the garage of an anonymous terraced house identical to thousands of others around it. The hostage was moved from his backseat to the bed of the house's laundry room, four-by-ten-foot and completely covered in polystyrene panels.

Sante and I left Luciano and Luigi to guard the swine. An hour later, the car was belching large bubbles as it disappeared into the murky brown waters of a canal.

That same night I was already on my way home in a stale, smoke-filled carriage on the national railroad.

It hadn't gone as I'd expected. Until then I'd only seen a swine in chains, pathetic creatures stinking of urine, sweat, and fear, like babies whimpering at a medicine they didn't want to take.

Irritating, not moving.

This time I had entered his home, been among his things. I had smelled the swine's intimacies, sensed his feelings. I had violated his affections.

This time had been different, painfully so.

The swine, despite living too well, according to our sources, didn't live a life of excessive luxury. The house was clean, welcoming, happy.

He had thought of his family and not of himself. He had not begged for mercy. His daughters kept photos beside their beds; their clothing comfortable, not extravagant. They had looked at us with hatred, not with contempt.

What right had we to enter their home? Why should they have to share their belongings with us? Why were we stealing their father and husband? Was it their fault that we were who we had become?

In the morning, as usual, all doubt and remorse had vanished. I got off the train and went home. I happily shared the news with my father: the swine was ours.

He showed no enthusiasm.

He had changed lately. I saw it in his silent reproaches, in his insistence that the family subside on his small but reliable government salary. The money I'd recently brought home was safe in a big glass jar buried in the garden. Even the queens had stopped begging for their presents. They had grown up and were beginning to understand. Everyone disapproved of us now.

Luciano and I were convinced we had saved them. We loved them immensely, he as much as I, and we were happy to have afforded them an easier life and, above all, the freedom to feel as they pleased. One day they would come to appreciate us.

We had protected my sisters—they would not share the fate of so many sweet village girls. They would not be spirited away, tearfully waving from the passenger seat of a roaring Fiat 124 special-T with a stupid fluffy dog by their side, by some *ciaonè* fleeing back to the North.

They would not meet the end of so many other southern girls who fell for skinny kids from the North, friends of emigrant factory workers who came down for the summer holidays. Every August, the sorry souls would arrive in shiny new Fiats bought on loan, spinning miraculous tales in Italian—the only language they spoke—about their wonderful lives in the city: how they went out for pizza every Saturday and spent Sundays at the cinema. Not to mention the occasional weekend jaunt. They would ensnare the splendid and naïve village girls and marry them after flash engagements, claiming they had many commitments and no time to waste. In the process, they avoided having to reveal too much about themselves.

During these syncopated periods of courtships, we'd see swarms of girls on the arms of the most improbable lovers, promenading with their fabulous finds; and yes, maybe he wasn't much to look at, but what an extraordinary life he could offer his future wife.

They greeted everyone with a flippant *ciao né*, which was where they got their nickname. In reality, the men broke their backs working six days a week in the factories and stayed home on Sundays to wash their own clothes. They were preposterous to modern and savvy city girls, so instead they chased after our girls, claiming that they were looking for the kind of seriousness in a woman that one could only find in the South. As a token of appreciation, they would bring chocolates and candies for the kids. They would spend a summer month with their factory friends, who would take them around to relatives, singing the praises of these boys who had a permanent job, and some unlucky girl would always fall for it.

We kids hated them, the *ciaonè*. Shockingly ugly, they would go off with the most beautiful girls in the village. After a few years, the girls would come home for the summer alone, without their *ciaonè*—who always stayed home to work overtime—sagging from childbearing and fatigue, pale and weather-beaten from damp houses in ghettos on the industrialized outskirts of the city.

The poor girls didn't have the courage to leave, and could only whisper through tears to the other girls who received new marriage proposals that it was "better to be a spinster at home." No, my sisters would avoid that misfortune, they would not end up wringing out the underwear of some metalworker, raising his snot-nosed kids. Nor would they be crammed into public housing with a pair of brats clinging to their skirts, after warming up the meal and the bed of some northern engineer, like Minna Bonasira had.

If only the cursed Milanese councilman had shown up twenty years earlier to bring jobs to the Aurora.

My father had resigned himself to losing me since my birth, when he had heard the midwife announce five times that I was a girl, her stubborn attempt to avert the Evil Eye she was certain had been fixed on me. Each time, he bit back his bitterness and replied, "as long as she's healthy." What else could he say?

After I told him the kidnapping had been successful, he was tormented all night.

He'd spoken to Sante and, with a heavy heart, he did what he had to do.

We would pay the price for all the evil we had done and were about to do. My father would suffer irreparably. Luciano's punishment would be harsh. Luigi, in keeping with his weak nature, would chose to save himself and sell human flesh.

But the one responsible for everything that had already

happened and that was yet to come, its instigator and true author, was me.

Convinced I was saving them, I led them to perdition.

Based on his prior experience, Sante was convinced that the right time to move the hostage was one week after the kidnapping.

Sante explained that once the alarm was sounded, the police would develop three possible scenarios: the hostage would be sent to the Aspromonte, to Tuscany, or he would stay in the area. In case the first hypothesis was the correct one, the police would monitor all the Calabrian junctions; the second, those of Tuscany; and the third, they'd visit all the previous offenders in the area. If the first phase was unsuccessful, they'd change tack around the one-month mark. They'd pretend to ease up on their inspections, hoping that if the hostage hadn't already been moved, his captors would use the chance to move him to less agitated waters. We had to avoid the first week after capture and the end of the month, but they couldn't check millions of people and vehicles. They'd have to limit themselves to highway exits and activate their army of informants.

So in the late afternoon of the seventh day after the crime, a large truck belonging to a shipping company near Linate airport took the west ring road to the motorway heading south, loaded with nothing more than furniture and vestments destined for a church in Catania, or so said the bill of lading. Three people sat on a hard bench at the back of the trailer like passengers on a train. One wore a black woolen hood that covered his face.

The riders in question were Luciano, Luigi, and the businessman.

The driver in the cab was an elderly Sicilian man on the verge of retirement. He drove calmly, careful never to exceed the speed limits on that particular trip.

Without having faced a single setback in ten hours, he stopped for a few seconds at a rest stop on the Salerno-Reggio Calabria highway and let off three passengers, his heaviest load. Thus unburdened, he would go on his way to Catania.

Who would have ever imagined kidnappers would walk forty miles through the woods?

There were no brigands anymore. The cops didn't even contemplate the scenario and instead were snoozing in the fields near the highway exits.

The hostage was lucky, he had a tender swineherd—my father—who had built him a clean, decent shelter, completely different from the usual pigsties. He was chained up just the same, but he had a gas heater, a camping lamp during the day, books, a mattress on a cot, and lots of soft, clean blankets. He had water and plenty of food.

It wasn't as comfortable as state-run prisons like Asinara or Pianosa where we wayward shepherds often ended up, but all in all he couldn't complain.

After our nighttime walk, we went down to the village. We would return to the mountains in high summer.

First, like the other students, we faced our exams, sweaty and pale. Luciano took care of the written exams for everyone. For our orals Luigi and I depended on the good hearts of the committee members. Luciano, as usual, outdid himself. The skeptical committee chairman, who had a degree in physics, saw the high marks the Institute had awarded the boy and felt it necessary to ask him about an obscure theorem. To the astonishment of the external committee, and the pride of our late Professor Augusto Mammì, Luciano not only cited the theorem, but wrote out the proof in three pages. When the chairman recovered, a few months later, he wrote an extremely humble and moving letter imploring Luciano to go study physics, even suggesting a famous teacher to approach, whom the chairman himself had already contacted. This demonstrates what good people worked in our schools back then, how they placed the welfare of the students before everything, even themselves.

We managed scores of a low sixty, an unexpected fifty, and an encouraging thirty-six. We received our diplomas and left for a happy holiday in the mountains, our last for many years.

We found a party that we never could have imagined, considering that my father and Bino had never been celebratory types. One man required half an hour to reproduce his own stunted signature; the other made do with a cross he could scratch out in half a second. And now, go figure, they had three high school graduate sons, since both considered themselves fathers to all three of us.

They had slaughtered a goat, the most beautiful wether, the pride of the herd, and we could already smell its aroma. Pleased and slightly bewildered, we let ourselves celebrate and went to bed happy and astounded. My father even brought a nice full plate to the swine; I saw him sneak off, lighthearted, in the direction of the pigsty where he kept the hostage.

Bino was so happy that after years of reticence he finally emptied his shriveled goiter. He told us about the great shit-smearing of 1935 and why he had resigned from the honorable society, retiring in good order.

Everyone knew the society of *pungiuti* had been an invention of the immoral Bourbons who had ruled Naples in the eighteenth century. The shrewd Spaniards understood that to shore up their power and contain the riotous peoples dispersed over hundreds of tiny mountain villages, the people of the forest, they would need more than just their bayonets; they would need to rely on natives to control their own people.

So they sent Spanish knights, mystic guardians of ancient codes, to prick fingers and found brotherhoods around the Kingdom, secret brotherhoods of honorable men who patrolled their own villages and kept their own people in line. Every subsequent regime would rediscover the usefulness of this system, invoking the secret societies as a form of invisible control. The Kaiser of Predappio was the first to stop the practice, since fascism imposes consensus with a whip, or worse. During the twenty years of Mussolini's regime, it was common to witness beatings of *malandrini*, who tasted the truncheon and confinement as often as their heroic dissident companions.

One iron rule of the brotherhood was that the honorable members modeled honorable behavior, and that they avoided bringing shame upon the society by tolerating unfaithful mothers, sisters, and daughters. When a forbidden affair in the village was revealed, as long as the cuckold was a common man, pranksters would hang a nice pair of goat horns on the unfortunate victim's door. He in turn would stay up all night waiting for the event, in order to make the horns disappear as quickly as possible.

If an honorable member had been cuckolded, however, or if a relative of his had been, the society would immediately strip him of his duties, which was tantamount to an immediate dismissal. The ensuing ritual required a senior *malandrino* to confront the cuckolded brother in a public street, in broad daylight, and smear a fistful of manure in his face, declaring him no longer worthy of belonging to the honorable society. The shit-smeared member would accept, wash himself of the disgrace with blood or, when this was impossible, with a long rehabilitation period, after which he was readmitted to the secret rites.

In 1935, when Don Salvuccio Guastella, the village doctor, passed away, the fascist hierarch at the time was Comrade

Sante Tropeano, who was more accustomed to telling jokes than to administering the truncheon or castor oil.

The only scion of the richest family in the countryside, Salvuccio grew bored of easy city skirts and, having comfortably obtained a degree in medicine at the University of Rome, returned to the village at forty years of age. As a country doctor he attended to both the local maladies and the village's impregnable thighs.

In truth, his conquests didn't have as much to do with his charm, which was waning, as they did the villagers' hunger. As everyone knows, all over the world in times of misery, women are the ones who bring home the bread.

One of the only sources of work in town was the Bourbon palace that occupied nearly all of Piazza San Sebastiano, and the extensive estates belonging the Guastella family. Many were the women who tended to the needs of the elderly confirmed bachelor.

Guastella's servants were regularly replaced. In the darkest periods, in exchange for some extra bread, many of them fell before the irresistible conqueror. The shrewdest observers whispered that half the countryside had descended from Guastella. The husbands of the women in service to him were filled with terror at the prospect of recognizing the doctor's features in their own children.

However, the Don Juan hadn't been in action for some thirty years, and everything had been forgotten by the morning of October 13, 1935, when, at the age of ninety-five, still virile by all indications, his death was announced by his trusted servant.

The entire countryside attended Don Salvuccio's funeral, the departed having been its richest and most illustrious inhabitant. Only a few impertinent elders let out a snicker during Don Remigio's eulogy at the priest's affirmation that the deceased had been like a father to his fellow countrymen.

Don Salvuccio was buried, and everyone eyed his mansion and his grounds. It would all go to the state, with the Guastellas now extinct.

After a few months passed and nobody thought about it anymore, a group of villagers were summoned to the town hall for an important announcement. The invitations had been stamped by Royal Notary Mr. Egidio Notarbartolo, and a total of seventeen men and women were to appear.

The mystery of the announcement was soon resolved. On his own initiative, Don Salvuccio had recognized all of his mules in his will and testament.

People fainted, especially since two had been joined in holy matrimony and had had numerous children. Seven of the mules comprised the entire leadership of the honored society, the official shit-smearer and boss included.

Guastella was very generous when he died, and all of his possessions, which were considerable for those parts, were divided equally among his bastard children; the revelation of the dishonor was buried by acres of pastures, farmhouses, vineyards, olive presses, and large sums of cash. The new orphans left arm in arm, knowing half the village was family. And they would squander all their abundant well-being in a flash.

Their legal problems were soon resolved; the Holy Rota annulled the incestuous union.

A few days after the will was unsealed, people's attention turned to the *malandrini*. They had all been the products of affairs. Notary certified affairs. Their changed economic conditions attested to their acceptance of their status.

And who could say anything, since they were the most ruthless members of the organization?

The *picciotti* subordinates wouldn't dream of smearing manure in the faces of their leaders. The pranksters didn't have the courage to enact the treatment on the non-*malandrini* bastard stepchildren, either, since they were still close relatives of the honored brothers, even if they were the products of cuckolding.

So the *pungiuti* made their rounds in peace. Seven brothers, who had made a blood oath and were now actual blood brothers, forgot about the Spanish rules and the humiliations inflicted on honorable members like them.

Only one prankster was young and foolish enough to have the courage to honor the tradition: Sante Tropeano.

The hard part was finding the trophy horns that marked a *cornuto*, a cuckold. In those miserable times it wasn't easy to find so many beasts ready to be sacrificed all at once.

His comrades of the Agrigentino, where more goats

were bred than anywhere else in the South, answered his call, arriving in Piazza San Sebastiano with a military truck escorted by a large squad of soldiers in fascist uniform, the Sons of the Wolves, as they were known.

Relieving the envy of the children whose mothers had kept their thighs closed tight against Salvuccio's graces and goodwill, the sons of the new Empire hung horns, harvested from what must have been enormous wethers, on the doors of the children born of Guastella's maids, or on doors of the women's cuckolded widowers, if they were still alive. And Sante and his pals left huge heaps of manure at the front doors of the seven honorable members.

The *pungiuti*, having swallowed their toad, awaited the collapse of the Empire, when Sante's fascist friends could no longer come to his aid. When they finally showed up at Tropeano's house to settle the account, all they found was an open barrel full of manure. Sante was on a ship bound for Argentina.

This was how Bino became disillusioned and broke away from the honorable and fallen society, dedicating himself to accompanying his noble goats.

The day after our graduation party, we loaded our backpacks and began our usual meandering. We spent days hiking among the beech and the larch trees on the highest part of the mountain. In early August, when we were hunting for brigand treasures in the caves of Malupassu, following a secret lead from Luciano, Bino tracked us down to announce that Sante had arrived.

He found Luigi and me lying on a sprawling gray parachute with Luciano reading us love letters, in English, that an allied paratrooper had left in a case with his uniform and documents at the back of an unexplored tunnel. We put everything back where we'd found it, to await the return of the now elderly aviator or his descendant. We fell in line behind Bino's brisk strides to return to the fold. Bino confirmed that the remains of old military aircraft were not infrequently found in that area. Some of them were empty, while others had become the coffins of wistful young pilots.

We found Sante in good spirits; he'd convinced Santoro to come south with his girlfriend. They were all staying together down the mountain, housed in one of the first residences built on the coast. He'd left them having lunch at my parents' house and had come to see us.

Everything was fine, he said. The negotiations for the ransom payment would soon be resolved. He was already working hard to find us accommodations in Milan, saying he wanted us all to be college graduates and enough with this fooling around. Until we found a place of our own, we would stay with him.

Everything had been quiet here, too, we explained; cops and *pungiuti* had visited the Aspromonte sheepfolds in vain, hoping for news about the hostage, or news of strange individuals carrying millions of lire. They had given up and left for Sardinia on a tip from Don Peppino Zacco, who assured them that barbarians from that island were the perpetrators.

Sante went away happy. He left behind his caliber 9, a military weapon that would have earned him at least five years in prison if they'd caught him with it, and in return he asked me for the Colt Cobra from Cavalier Fera.

It was all going a little too well.

We would never see Sante again, but when we said goodbye on that blue August day, he seemed so genuinely benevolent.

We quietly resumed our mountain holiday. The sea held no attraction for us, with its deserted sun-baked beaches, flat and bare as far as the eye could see. It wasn't for us.

Leaving the three of us behind at the fold each day, my father and Bino, radiant as they had been in recent times—and what a miracle that was—joyfully set off over the pasture with their sacks overflowing and their flasks full of wine. After years of cajoling, we had finally secured permission to renovate the goat paddock, and in the absence of my father's long-standing opposition, we rearranged the enclosure.

For three or four days, I watched my father and Bino head out for the pasture. Then I decided I would figure out their secret.

The next morning, I waited for their now predictable merry exit and quickly went ahead of them to wait in the pastures, armed with binoculars, leaving Luigi immersed in work on the enclosure, Luciano directing it.

After a while I caught a glimpse of them, my two goatherds, lying blissfully in the shadow of the enormous hackberry tree down in the Sardivia pits, a plateau the size of four soccer fields suspended between the mountains, as the goats tranquilly grazed.

My heart leapt to my throat as I spotted a figure approaching on their right. Just before a whistle of warning leapt from my tongue to my lips, I saw Bino rise slightly and nod to the newcomer.

My fear subsided into amazement. The man walked with an uncertain but calm step. He was holding the type of ax shepherds carried, but there was no chance he was a shepherd, his chest was too erect. Only then did I realize he was wearing camouflage; the label, now visible, read "Ejército Español." My camouflage.

The three of them ate peacefully, took a quiet nap, and then followed the goats to the river. I watched them for a time and returned to the sheepfold, where I found Luigi nailing boards while Luciano snoozed.

Our shepherds reappeared at dusk with a satisfied air, they praised our work, rushed through their chores, kissed all three of us, then got into the car to go down to the village.

That night I thought about the man who had approached Bino and my father under the hackberry tree. I concluded he'd been a shadow, a fugitive, whom they'd wanted to hide from us, too; it was not uncommon for them to give shelter to someone without mentioning a word about it, not even to me. Then came sleep. And in a dream I recognized him: he was anything but a shadow. His prominent shepherd's belly had fooled me. They'd fattened him up well. The crazy old geezers were letting our hostage roam free in the mountains.

I knew from experience that it wasn't unheard of as a practice, especially when the prisoners were with us for a long time. Some shepherds had even brought hostages to bathe in the sea or out to eat at a restaurant. It had also happened that hostages with stingy relatives had on occasion been released before their ransom was paid, agreeing to return to settle the bill for themselves once everything had calmed down.

"Stories," I told myself, thinking my two shepherds would have sensed I was onto them.

But they didn't sense anything. They arrived early the following morning, rousing us, as excited as children home from school. They were bearing a huge tray of sweets, which Sante had sent him, they said, plus two giant amberjacks to grill, a gift from a fisherman friend who had "stayed awake all night to fish" and, miracle of progress, a cooler as high as Bino's groin, full of beer and ice cream.

How could I spoil that joy?

Unaware of my concerns, Luigi and Luciano were already gorging themselves.

I looked at the faces of the shepherds, at the encouragement in their eyes, and dove into the party.

They waited for us to collapse from our binge and went off with a loaded donkey to look for their goats and the swine.

I watched them in secret for a few more days. I observed how respectful the hostage was with Bino, the long conversations he had with my father. No, he wasn't duping them, I thought. He had been free perhaps for months, yet every day he showed up to their appointment on time.

He had made a pact on his honor, I told myself.

Later, I understood: my father had finally found a friend; Bino had found that God had seen fit to grant him another adopted son at his venerable age.

The Milanese entrepreneur had rekindled their consciences, which had been dormant, not dead.

The last days of August arrived, and the spell was broken. A sorry Marshal Palamita was the bearer of the bad news.

The village was an oven. The unbearable heat had driven Bino and my father to seek refuge in the mountains, and they had been staying in the sheepfold.

The marshal arrived in his Fiat Campagnola, leaving his fellow officer in the car. His stride was unusually slow. His face wore a solemn expression.

Bino foresaw misfortune and to dispel it said, "Boys, get a coffee for the marshal."

It was useless. The evil could not be undone. Sante had been dead for two days. He'd been eating breakfast with his family when two hired assassins burst in; everyone in the area knew Sante and no one had had the courage to do the job themselves.

The fools had anticipated an easy job. Sensing an ambush, Sante unloaded five rounds from his Colt Cobra. He was still reloading when the other two assassins standing on guard outside checked the house after their friends didn't emerge.

Sante didn't reload in time, and he paid for the twenty years' worth of toads he had forced the *pungiuti* to swallow. The assassins were so shocked to find Sante alive that they only managed to hit him once, and though the village hospital couldn't save him, his killers didn't have the courage to celebrate. They denied all involvement.

Anna had already taken Sante away to be buried in Milan.

We could only mourn over his photos.

The blackest soul, the terror of the *pungiuti*, was gone. But in the shadows, an even blacker one was already growing.

We cried for a month. The pain was immense. So it was we came to understand the suffering of others, of mothers, wives, children. But in the end, as always, life took the upper hand.

We stalled for a few more weeks. We had no direct experience negotiating a kidnapping ransom, nor did we even want the money—we did not want to profit off of what had been

Sante's idea. We wanted to clear his conscience of that last wicked act.

Finally we left everything up to Bino and my father, who were overjoyed at being able to send the hostage back to his family.

They had been taking care of the fold with Leonardo, as they'd been calling him for months. He wore the white shirt and black pants of a shepherd, he climbed into the jeep with the two cousins, and together they took the dirt road, with its curves and potholes, down to the town.

He looked like any other villager when he took a seat in a cramped and stale carriage on the national rail train bound for the North.

Leonardo disembarked in Florence, caught a bus that connected the city to the mountain villages, got off with a bag in his hand, took a walk in the woods, changed his clothes, and then, appropriately disheveled and confused, knocked on the door of the first house he saw to beg for help.

The next day he appeared on the news, unrecognizable from the long months of deprivation. He was wearing a Benemérita jacket over a tattered cashmere coat. A military T-shirt with "Ejército Español" written on it peeked through his open shirt.

The strong grip of the law—which was currently off chasing down savage Sardinian shepherds—had distracted Leonardo Brambilla's torturers just long enough for the wealthy Milanese industrialist to escape without paying the billion-lire ransom demanded of his family.

Our paths would cross again.

We arrived in Milan on November 2, the Day of the Dead. We settled into a boarding house on viale Abruzzi, number 17. We left our luggage, and after a quick shower found the tram stop on viale Piave. The 29 left us in front of the Monumentale Cemetery, the eternal resting place of distinguished Milanese.

The socialist councilman had procured a plot for Sante's black soul. We asked for the location of the headstone and went to visit. A blond boy was standing near it, hand in hand with a girl, and he blew kisses in the direction of Sante's photo before walking away.

We stood where the two kids had been. Sante was an innocent boy again in the photo, which portrayed him in younger years. Below the photo, Anna had ordered an inscription: "You lived and died by your own rules, leaving your wife, your son, and your brothers to mourn your absence."

It was too much. We ran away. We didn't even leave the flowers we'd bought at the entrance, dropping them instead at the door of some fancy chapel.

Anna had loved Sante while he was alive and understood him in his death.

———

On the 5th of November, the last possible day to register for university classes, I enrolled in medicine, Luigi in economics, and Luciano, after having been admitted to the physics department, chose law, to the displeasure of many a former teacher.

On the basis of our income, our tuition and accommodations were subsidized. In December, we moved into three single rooms in a student dormitory on viale Romagna. The dorm was like a seaport, or an Arabian souk. A microcosm of assorted humanity crowded the halls, the canteen, the study rooms. British students, Americans, Arab scholarship kids, aspiring terrorists, budding geniuses. In other words, the future.

Junkies, thieves, maniacs, they all passed through. A constant party. It stunned us for a while. Our Valenciano days were over; you couldn't just leave twenty thousand lire on a woman's nightstand. She would have throttled you.

We led a life of leisure. After a year I had passed one exam, Luciano had passed seven, and Luigi hadn't passed any.

I found a large glass jar containing most of the money we'd robbed from the owner of the Valenciano in the suitcase my mother had packed for me before I left. Thirty-six million lire, shared between Luciano and me, now sat in the air duct that lead to my room, protected by three Beretta 9x19-caliber pistols.

The university grants were awarded on a rigid merit-based system: if you took all your exams, you got to keep everything. If you partied too much, you lost it all. No accommodations, stipend, canteen or book discount.

After a year, Luigi and I had decidedly lost it all.

We sublet two other rooms for no small price in the same student dorm and continued to make withdrawals from the jar. After another year, I had managed to pass one more exam, Luigi passed none, while Luciano doubled his total from the year before.

We had fifteen million lire left. A trafficker claimed eight to educate Luigi, who, having passed no exams, succumbed to the unrelenting call to arms. Having passed another exam, I managed to postpone suspension for a year.

After two years we had seven million lire left and among the three of us had passed a total of sixteen exams.

Other students enjoyed this university period; they were adaptable and happy to do all kinds of odd jobs; it was normal, a fun experience for them.

We, on the other hand, with pasts in our pockets that were even heavier than our futures, what were we supposed to do? Get jobs at a bar serving customers with big trays of drinks and wait for the day some punk showed up to tell us who we were, to remind us of our sins? Were we supposed to whistle like Totò the Blade as we closed the bar?

Luciano immersed himself in the tortuous tangles of law. To avoid distractions, he'd gotten himself a steady girlfriend like the Milanese did. Meanwhile, Luigi and I began to keep ourselves occupied.

We were spoiled for choice on how to make money. We knew everyone in that seaport, their vices included.

We started dealing weed, and kids started to show up at our rooms to buy. We had a mule who would go down on the train once a month to visit our growers in the village. But it was just a little here and there to get by.

Self-destruction was in vogue at the time in Milan—the yuppy takeover was still a few years off. People wanted to escape life, not live it intensely. Kids were begging for heroin, that's where the real business was; everyone just wanted to sleep and we started to help them.

I went to see the Sicilian I'd met with Sante in Milan and introduced myself again.

"Meat in mouth and there's no problem," he said.

I didn't understand the expression.

"Cash up front," he said in dialect.

I returned to him with one bag and left with a different one. In six months we went from selling a hundred grams a week to a kilo. Cash started to roll in. We'd moved up from the junkies to the small-time pushers. And then came the turning point. A pusher came looking for us.

Khaled—a Syrian student, a political refugee, a robust, athletic, and gregarious guy—began to seek me out. He didn't look Middle Eastern or speak with the inflection of the Arabs. He clung to me like a tick, and he did so much business with us he became our partner and our brother. After a few months of hanging around us, he even began to speak our dialect. We introduced him as our *paesano*, our friend from home, and everyone found him irresistible.

We'd see Luciano every few weeks or so, but he wouldn't even open the door for us when we called on him, busy with his woman and his books. So Luigi and I spent all our time with Khaled, whom we began to call Salvatore, or Sasà for short.

When Luciano found out we were trafficking, his infatuation with the straight life suddenly vanished. "I gave up women and school. What are you up to?"

"This," said Luigi, pressing a hundred grams of horse into his hand.

Luciano had seen Sasà around but hadn't realized how close we'd all become. Now he understood, and the four of us were inseparable.

After a few months, Luciano took me aside to talk about Sasà. "I don't know," he said. "He's growing on me, but I have a funny feeling about him."

I told him he might be right, that maybe we'd gone too fast, but he was just hanging out with us. He was sharp, useful—he didn't make a fuss about whose job it was to do what.

"Maybe you're just jealous!" I said, giving him a jab. We laughed it off and forgot about it.

Sasà was always laughing; you could hear his laughter before you saw him. Sometimes Luciano would even scold him when he seemed to be making fun of people.

At one point, he went away for a few weeks to see his

relatives, refugees in Germany. When he returned he spoke to us in a serious tone, without laughing.

"Do you want to move even more dope?" he asked us.

Not long after, we were handling monthly shipments of a ton each, working directly with the Gray Wolves, the Turkish paramilitaries.

We would play a fundamental role in the Milan of the roaring '80s, the Milan of judicial ruins. Countless people would come to us from Calabria, Sicily, Naples—policemen, entrepreneurs, politicians, and magistrates.

We thought we were sharpshooters, the straightest of them all; we had plunged ourselves into darkness to make room for a bright future. In actuality, we'd voluntarily enlisted in someone else's war. We were selling death and someone else was making money on it. But we knew what we were doing. We had been arming ourselves since we were young in order to be free. Now we were still armed but had become all too similar to those we had originally set out to fight.

We didn't go seeking the Turkish drug connection; the drugs had come looking for us. By the time I understood why, it was too late. Luciano had guessed the truth—he'd warned me but I hadn't believed him, and as usual I dragged him into it along with me.

We thought we were shining stars. In truth we were angels of darkness.

SHADOWS
IN LIGHT

Sasà would often disappear for a few days at a time, returning as if nothing had happened, as if he had been studying the whole time. On one of these occasions I went to his room to pay him a visit.

We chatted a little, then he picked up an envelope and pulled out a sheet of paper. "Do you know Vincenzo Sparta?" he asked.

Don Vincenzo's door was only half-closed. The huge hall, its air heavy with ancient odors, was dimly illuminated by wall lamps.

I crossed the floor and started up the stairs under the sad gaze of Donna Agata, Sparta's late wife, who scrutinized me severely from a portrait on the wall. It was said Donna Agata had died a virgin, that her husband, the most author-itative godfather in all Calabria, had been impotent—that she had adored her husband so much she had taken the blame for his lack of heirs. I looked down and didn't look up again until I'd reached the landing. There was a room in front of me, its door open wide, and at the far end, a large window opened onto a narrow veranda choked with bougainvillea. A cool breeze redolent with wet jasmine caressed my face.

It smelled of peace—the kind that follows a bloody battle.

The ancient man sat halfway between the veranda and me, hunched over his desk. He was over ninety years old and never spent more than a few months as a revered guest in a federal penitentiary, despite his many crimes; he had sidestepped major legal imbroglios by keeping lawyers and senators in his pocket for half a century. He represented the history and myth of my land. Now, in his old age, he had become fixated on writing, and spent entire days hunched over his desk. It seemed as though he would die of old age without paying for the evil he'd done.

My rubber billy club sank mercifully into the patriarch's nape, and his chin drooped into his writing as if he had fallen into a sudden sleep, as the elderly are wont to do.

I glanced at his writings: brief, concise thoughts, little more than notes. His calligraphy was elegant, almost solemn.

Quickly, I gathered up the boss's manuscript and pen, substituting them with replacements I had brought with me. I lifted him and propped his head against the back of the chair.

I climbed over the balcony railing and my feet found the rungs of the ladder that Luciano had already positioned against the wall.

I took the sawed-off Bernardelli shotgun from my bag and pulled both triggers together, joylessly. Eighteen pellets of buckshot sprayed the face of Don Vincenzo, nearly beheading him and returning him to his Creator on that cool and fragrant summer evening.

In less than an hour, we were on the highway heading north. I drove, and Luciano sat next to me with a flashlight, reading the old man's memoirs. I had promised Sasà that I would destroy everything without reading it, and in fact I never read a word. We sped along, Luciano enjoying the company of a deceased boss, while I enjoyed a very much alive rock-and-roll boss, as "Born to Run" blared over the radio.

On nights like these, the highway was full of children of the forest—thousands of people from our town and many other towns like ours, towns that had once sat on the summits of the Aspromonte, only to have been rebuilt in the foothills or by the sea. We filled the lanes with our powerful cars, crisscrossing the peninsula and the continent. We were all the same, moving at a breakneck speed, like birds of prey freed from our mountain cages. We invaded the service areas, groups of young people buying one another coffee, embracing, and exchanging addresses. We thoughtlessly risked tragedy, convinced we would conquer the world. Instead, we were robbing ourselves of a future.

That evening Luciano and I didn't stop at the service areas to greet the other boys. We couldn't allow ourselves to be seen. We had never taken that trip. We didn't even stop for gas; we filled our tank with cans we'd stored in the trunk.

Lost in my own thoughts, I drove without noticing the time. Just as we passed the sign for Attigliano, the gas light came on.

As I pulled over, Luciano clutched my shoulder, his nails digging into my skin. I looked at him for the first time since we'd been in the car and froze: he was pale, sweating.

"What's wrong?" I asked.

He ripped three strips of paper from the manuscript and got out of the car. He filled up the tank, doused the notebooks with the remaining gasoline, and set them on fire. When he got back in the car, I could see he wasn't sick, he was terrified.

"We're fucked," he said. "We should turn this car around and disappear into our mountains. Forget this ever happened."

I set off again, then slowed down to take the next exit before changing my mind and putting my foot back on the accelerator. Luciano slouched down in the passenger seat and slept soundly until we reached Milan.

Back in the city, we went to bed. The next afternoon we met with Luigi and Sasà. We took a stroll around the city center and in the evening we dined at the Frassino, one of the most luxurious local restaurants. We stayed up late and went home happy, as we always were when we were together.

Before we went to bed, Sasà mentioned that he would be gone for a few days.

"You've heard all the news," Luigi said.

But there was more news, because the next morning Sasà came to wake me. He gave me forged documents by which I became Luca Marra, and he, Xavier Ordonnez. A car, which had a Spanish license plate from Almeria, was waiting for us under a chestnut tree on viale Romagna.

For the first time in my life, I crossed the Italian border. Actually, I crossed two borders on a single journey.

We arrived in Spain and went south, through Girona, Barcelona, Tarragona, Castellón, Valencia, Murcia, and Almería. I was as excited as a kid at an amusement park. In Badora, we left the highway and drove into the Sierra Nevada, whose peaks were well above ten thousand feet.

How I wished Luciano were with me.

We arrived later that evening in Larcal, a small village of shepherds located at the top of a rocky ridge at an altitude of almost seven thousand feet. "Xavier" confidently navigated the narrow streets of the village and parked behind a small white house on the edge of the town. He proceeded to open the car door and loudly called out, "Alberto!" A light flicked on and a little man came out to meet us. He hugged Xavier tightly, then shook my hand. We declined his offer of food and we all went to bed.

I felt like I had only just closed my eyes when the smiling shepherd appeared at the door holding a tray with coffee. As soon as we tasted it, I opened my backpack and retrieved my Italian percolator and coffee.

That day we would climb up to our host's sheepfold, eat in the mountains, and return in the evening. I heaved the backpack with the necessary supplies for the day onto my shoulders and we went out into the darkness of the Sierra. We began to climb a trail that I immediately intuited was treacherous. I saw the smile on Alberto's face and understood. He was playing a game with us that I had played dozens of times in the Aspromonte, a favorite of lonely mountain folk when they thought they were in the company of inexperienced city people. It consisted of walking at a brisk pace, too brisk for even a mountaineer, for about half a mile. The guide would chat and joke around as if the gait were a leisurely walk while the victim tried to prove himself, clenching his teeth and losing his footing. Inevitably, he would start gasping, his legs would seize up, and the walk would become an ordeal. At that point, the mountaineer would resume his normal gait, but the hierarchies would be established.

Alberto launched himself ahead of us, whistling happily.

He looked straight ahead, waiting for us to fall far behind him and beg for mercy. He never had to turn around, though, because his acute mountain senses told him that I was right on his tail. When we reached that half-mile mark when the game should have ended, he gritted his teeth and continued, chuckling to himself. When we had gone another few hundred feet, he whirled around and looked at me. "What mountains are you from?" he demanded. We hugged each other and resumed at a more merciful pace.

It grew lighter, and I began to observe the landscape, which was beautiful, though the trees didn't tower gigantically and the brush only came up to our ankles. The climb was hard but the ground was smooth; despite their altitude, these were easy mountains.

We crossed a clearing covered with seedlings that I identified with horror as oregano. It had no aroma and was one-fifth as tall as ours. In our dialect, everything that was smaller, or less beautiful, or less difficult than what we were accustomed to, we referred to as *malgioglio*. After taking it in all day, I defined the entire Sierra Nevada as *malgioglio*.

When we arrived at the fold, I was not surprised to find a flock of sheep; this was no place for goats. I enjoyed myself all the same, helping Alberto milk the beasts, curd the cheese, and cook ricotta.

Men in camouflage, some twenty in all, began to emerge from the forest in pairs; they hugged Sasà, exchanged a few words in Arabic, and greeted me with a slight bow.

They were all young, between the ages of twenty and thirty, except for one bearded man in his forties. They were armed with guns that I identified from their kicks as Llama 9x19 mm Parabellums and heavy French assault rifles, Famas 223-caliber Remingtons.

We sat down together to eat milk and ricotta. They joked around with Sasà, who answered their questions through fits of laughter. After we finished breakfast, Sasà left with the eldest of the group, and the others, having overcome their shyness, began to bombard me with questions. Some spoke Italian and acted as interpreters for the rest. They had a thousand curiosities, starting with football, then followed by women, cinema, fashion. They were simple, warm people, but also soldiers in top physical form.

My understanding with Alberto was perfect; he left to take the flock to the pasture, leaving me to be master of the kitchen. I sacrificed a young lamb to fill our many mouths. The boys looked at me curiously while I quickly killed, skinned, and butchered the lamb, which ended up in a large pot. Two tomatoes, two peppers, some onions, basil, salt, and oil. After forty-five minutes over the fire, the meat was done.

We had a happy lunch and a happy day, and that evening we regretfully took our leave. I gave the boys my backpack full of pasta, coffee, sugar, peeled tomatoes and other Italian products. They stayed behind in the woods, waving us off.

We were euphoric upon our return to Milan, bearing the news everyone had been waiting to hear. Sasà explained that most of the work was done; the two of us had to take one last trip together, while Luciano and Luigi would start contacting all our boys from back home to secure their availability. We would start in a few weeks.

Using another set of forged documents, we landed at Heraklion Airport after a stopover in Athens. We rented a small off-road vehicle and headed toward Sitia, in the eastern part of Crete. We drove up to Olos, another village of shepherds. We climbed a narrow dirt road that ended in another fold, this time with goats.

The goatherd's name was Dimitri, but he was actually an Arab, too. He and Sasà conversed for a few hours and were visibly satisfied when they said their goodbyes.

"Now all we have to do is wait," Sasà told me in the car.

We returned to Italy by ferry and reached Milan by train. We rented two apartments under borrowed names, one in the Corvetto area and one near Corso Sempione. And we waited.

Sasà would occasionally make a few calls from the public payphone; Luciano, Luigi, and I would wait in a line in front until he would silently step out. The children of the forest who came to ask us for news became increasingly disappointed each day we waved them off.

In those days, everyone wanted heroin, the "dark stuff." There were thousands of kids hanging around who were trying to annihilate themselves. The heroin market was divided into a thousand streams, with the biggest dealers moving twenty, thirty kilos a month at most. They were all supplied by small Turkish traffickers who, as Sasà explained, were actually Kurds with Turkish passports. They charged prices of fifty, fifty-five million lire a kilo on the first pass. The goods were often of low quality, and the supply wasn't continuous. If we could provide quality, price, and continuity, we would be able to control everything.

And in the end, the dark stuff arrived; after twenty days the great moment came. This time, when Sasà stepped out of the phone booth, we could barely keep up with him.

We rented a van with more false documents and bought a dozen enormous bags. The next day the four of us entered a shed belonging to a small engineering company in Brianza. We came out with two hundred kilos of dark stuff of a quality that, we later discovered, had never been seen before on the market.

The Turks charged us forty million a kilo. We had a debt of eight billion lire on our shoulders. "Two billion a head," Luigi calculated quickly. Instead of scaring us, the pressure just served as motivation.

We worked exclusively with Calabrians. Directly, one transfer only. People whose histories and families we knew. Safe people. We moved the stuff at forty-five million, earning five points per package. We wiped out the competition in a flash.

It was a potent product, one-five, one-six, meaning we could cut one kilo five or six times. Unprecedented potency.

After the first two weeks we'd run through over half of the goods, but had only collected four hundred million lire, which Sasà immediately brought to the Turks. Very few could pay us in advance; only the mob bosses paid in cash, using what they'd stashed away from kidnappings. The other Calabrians hadn't yet been able to distribute such large amounts of product.

Things changed in the third week. The boys returned in good spirits, with plastic bags full of money. Before the month was out, ahead of the agreed date, the Turks had collected the entire eight billion lire they'd requested; a week later we visited the Brianza company again to claim a load that was twice as big as the one before it.

We started to organize ourselves better. We rented several apartments in different neighborhoods. We had a dozen cars at the ready, with duplicate license plates belonging to unsuspecting motorists with no criminal records. We did the same with driver's licenses and personal identifications; from an official standpoint, we didn't exist. Neighborhood bars served as our offices. We'd choose one street and frequent all the bars on it so as not to disappoint anyone. We always met in person, without ever using the telephone. We chatted, we drank, and we'd establish the time and place of our subsequent meeting. Deliveries took place in a completely different area. We would occupy the same street for one or two months before moving on.

Processions of customers came to see us wherever we went. It wasn't long before people caught on, but when we paid the bill every night, the barman would find he'd collected double the cash he should have on the number of drinks we'd had. The bums who usually pestered the shops and the residents soon disappeared.

Milan loved us, and all the children of the forest like us. The city was too full of family men with their mortgages, promissory notes, bills to pay; it had everything to offer, but at a price. We met the needs of many, even among the boys in the Carabinieri or the federal police. Anyone who had a problem, economic or otherwise, found an answer in us, and we didn't even bother to keep track of all the loans we made.

The off-the-books industrial entrepreneurs, the folks raking in political kickbacks and the tax evaders would take their money to Switzerland, spending some of it in private circles. We helped them distribute their earnings around the city. The Calabrians flooded Milan with billions of lire, providing handouts to everyone. It was a long honeymoon.

The drug was death, and yet it wasn't considered a problem. Investigative units across all the agencies, absorbed for decades in anti-terrorist or anti-kidnapping activities, didn't even notice us; or, perhaps, as we later understood, they pretended not to.

Statistically, crime dropped. Robbers, kidnappers, cheats,

and scammers all converted to the drug trade, since no special skills or courage were required to pass a package from one hand to another and return home with full pockets.

They only worked during daylight, from Monday to Friday. In the evenings, the former goatherds could be found in restaurants, discos, and nightclubs. They were the best customers; they spared no expense, and certainly didn't limit themselves to pizza and a beer. Every group of boys who worked for us had an entourage of people from all walks of life.

We knew people in every part of the city. No one ever cared who you were, only how you dressed, what watch you wore, what car you drove, and how much cash padded your pockets.

We trafficked in death and distributed an average of a thousand kilos a month, which, after it was cut, meant five to six thousand kilos of dark stuff on the market and hundreds of billions of lire funneling into the city.

At our table sat politicians, magistrates, policemen, doctors, journalists, actors, and even a few clergymen. The list was endless.

And while part of the city wanted to die, an ever-growing segment wanted to live, and live large.

Our activities had been going at full sail for over a year when we began to frequent the bars on via San Marco. On our first day there, we had several important meetings. No one showed.

Luciano and I were sitting at a table, reading the newspaper. We saw two carabinieri enter, one with the rank of marshal and the other in a second lieutenant uniform. We weren't fazed; the carabinieri had never bothered us before.

For a moment the officer met my gaze. I bit my lip and lowered my eyes. I had made an unforgivable mistake. By nature, cops are similar to criminals. When you encounter one, you should avoid eye contact; otherwise you can read each other's souls. It won't matter if you are well dressed and well groomed and you look like a good boy. He can immediately see the evil in you.

As usual, we were carrying fake IDs and we were armed. I could feel the officer searching my mind. I kept my head down, but it was useless. As I'd known he would from the start, the second lieutenant approached our table, alone.

"Documents please, gentlemen." We handed them over without looking up at him. He read our names aloud and when he read our stated profession—Sales Representative—he did so with sarcasm.

I glanced toward the door. Luigi and Sasà were entering—some of the boys had warned them. They arranged themselves on either side of the marshal, who drank his aperitif in absolute tranquility by the bar.

"You look more like two stinking goatherds to me."

My blood stopped, and my hand jerked to the CZ-75 left to me by poor Sante.

"You think you're invisible, but I saw you today. Just like I saw you, Luciano, and Luigi by my father's grave on the Day of the Dead."

I looked up. It was Sante's son.

Luciano and I looked into his eyes, then we turned to Luigi and Sasà, who no longer knew what to do. They looked stunned as the three of us—big bruisers all, and cops and crooks to boot—were nearly moved to tears; only the marshal remained impassive.

My initial wave of emotion passed and I grew serious. "So what, are you a cop now?"

"Only in name," he replied.

"What about him?" I pointed to the marshal.

"The same."

They said they had things to do, so we said goodbye, planning to meet again later. That evening we all went to dinner together, except for Sasà, who had disappeared on one of his last-minute trips. Santoro told us how he became a *carabiniere*. After Sante's death, he'd felt lost, he didn't see us anymore, he didn't know anyone he could trust for certain things. He went through a hard time. He was convinced that he would have to execute his plans by himself, and joined the police force, reassured by the idea that he would be able to avenge his father that way—though he didn't plan to use his handcuffs when the time came.

"I thought you'd forgotten about my father, but then I heard about Don Vincenzo Sparta and instinctively I understood. Not even Sparta's closest confidants had any information about his death. It seemed to be a lone gun, and you guys are the kings of that kind of work."

He had been born and raised in the plains; we'd thought he was Milanese, but on the inside he was a son of the mountains like Sante, like us.

Sasà didn't know it, but his request that we do him the favor of killing Don Vincenzo had only accelerated a decision that had already been made regarding the old man's fate. The patriarch must have given his consent on Sante's murder; no one from our territory could have touched Sante without that permission. Don Vincenzo's blood was only the first that had to spill in order for me and Luciano to avenge Sante.

We could not forget him, nor did we wish to; he was the greatest black soul ever born in Aspromonte and his spirit flowed through our veins.

Understanding this, Santoro had spent a long time searching for us, in vain. He had found us by chance in the heart of Milan, a stone's throw from his office in Moscova. We were elusive shadows, even in broad daylight. We frequented the best establishments, we were the most visible people, and yet nobody knew who we really were. We were clandestine, but we lived alongside Milanese of every class. At any time we could have slipped our backpacks over our shoulders and disappeared back into the forest, never to be seen again. We had never really been there at all. We believed this, even as the city and its money tightened their knots around us. Oh, but we were there, of course we were, infusing the air with our stench, infesting the lives of others with our shit. We sold death and planned murders, speeding destructively toward an inevitable bullet or a set of handcuffs.

Santoro, as his father had done, assumed his mother's surname, which had been Milanese for generations, so no one suspected his past. He had married his blonde girlfriend from all those years before, the one we saw him grow up with, and who was now a judicial auditor at the municipal court.

We talked about everything with him, and without reservations; he was my blood, my cousin, the son of Sante Motta. Betrayal was not a part of his genetic code.

A few days after that meeting, we went to see Anna, Santoro's mother, who welcomed us like sons. She hadn't found herself another man, nor would she ever; she had filled the house with photos of Sante. She even had photos of us, from the Christmas holidays we'd spent in our mountains—there was one of the men, all drunk, including old Bino, my father, Sante, and the socialist councilman.

Anna knew what we liked to eat, and she sent us to pick up a goat she'd ordered from Peck. As we were about to sit down to dinner, the doorbell rang. It was the socialist councilman. He'd done well for himself. Now he was a member of parliament with a party undersecretary appointment, but that hadn't weakened his or his wife's relationship with Sante's family.

We raised the price of the dark stuff by one point per package to raise funds for Santoro and his faithful marshal. We maintained a cash pool among ourselves, and Luciano did the accounting, dividing proceeds into five equal parts: four for us, and one for Sasà's Arab friends, the guarantors who had made the whole operation possible. Our income grew into the billions, and we divided the cash among the various apartments we kept around the city.

After our meeting with Santoro, we intensified our relationship with the undersecretary, who invited us to attend the parties he often organized at his house. He introduced us to the Milan that mattered most in those days, gleefully presenting us to everyone as his collaborators. And one evening, at one of those parties, we ran into an old friend of ours.

A charming Spanish countess was expected to make an appearance. She was the owner of one of the most exclusive salons in Milan. She was on her second husband, a luminary cardiovascular surgeon, the owner of a prestigious Milanese clinic. When she made her entrance, a small retinue gathered around her, signaling her importance. The crowd cleared and Rino, our host, introduced us to the noblewoman. Her beauty was exotic, if not breathtaking, and suggested her exceptional abilities as a lover.

Donna Natalia greeted us impassively; only for Luigi did she allow a slight smile to appear on her lips, imperceptible to everyone else.

Obviously we weren't able to get her alone for even an instant during the party. When we said our farewells, she offered us her business card, to the astonishment of everyone present. It was extraordinary that Natalia would make herself so available after a first meeting. The probation period before entering into her good graces was usually much longer.

From time to time, we would run into her at some party, and very often we went to see her in private. The Andalusian Gypsy had come up in the world since the days of the Valenciano and her Sicilian pimp. We laughed heartily as we recounted the adventure on the express train to Milan. The pimp who had been relieved of such a large sum had never once suspected Natalia.

With her cut, she had taken over a bordello that had been an outlet for the cravings and vices of many important people. Then she had married the doctor, thus cloaking herself with a respectability that no one cared or dared to doubt, with all the people she had eating out of her hand. She hadn't given up the brothel—out of superstition, she said—but entrusted it to her business partner while she hopped from party to party.

She described in great detail that world, which was populated by all kinds of individuals. Few were truly rich, and most lived far above their means. Outsized homes, villas by the sea and in the mountains, lovers for him and her. All of them constantly on the verge of economic collapse. And she generously assisted them toward it, allowing them to offer her IOUs, blank checks, pledges, and mortgages.

We didn't explain our work to her, but we quantified our liquidity and she helped us organize it.

Right around the time of our reunion with Natalia, it happened that a boy from the Aurora, Tonino, who was younger than us, got arrested. We wasted no time in testing our relations with her.

Tonino had been caught by the narcotics squad while delivering thirty packages to the Neapolitans. The news caused an uproar; it was a huge seizure at the time. A preliminary forensics test confirmed that the powder in question was heroin of the brown sugar variety, with the highest percentage purity obtainable. Given the evidence and the flagrancy of the crime, Tonino and the Neapolitans were brought to trial within a matter of months.

At the request of the defense, the panel of judges ordered an expert report on the seized narcotics from a pharmacologist. The defense team appointed its own experts, and the hearing was deferred for the time necessary for the analysis to be completed.

Luciano and I stood among the crowd waiting to greet Tonino as he emerged from the courtroom. On the other side of the corridor were the narcotics team operatives who had conducted the seizure. As they stared us down with malicious, self-satisfied smiles, someone shouted an insult and a scuffle broke out. We managed to duck out before they could stop us and ask for our IDs.

We ran into the same officers at the next hearing, with their usual derisive air. This time, however, we had gotten the word out, and there were no other members of the public attending besides Luciano and me.

The court expert took his seat in front of the judges, stated his name and credentials, and was sworn in by the clerk. First, he described the method of the operations—the sampling of the packages seized, the type of analysis conducted, the reliability of said analysis, the number of repetitions—and came to the following conclusions: the substance consisted of a compound of fructose, glucose, rhubarb, and ginseng. A superficial analysis had detected a color, smell, and consistency similar to heroin but, scientifically speaking, the substance was completely free of the hallucinogenic and forbidden active ingredients. It was an easily metabolized product, excellent for low-calorie diets.

Tonino shouted from his cage: "Your Honor, I told the cops right away that I was trying to cheat the dealers."

The prosecutor, on the verge of a nervous breakdown, said: "I demand that the expert examination be repeated, with samples taken from all the packages in the presence of an expert appointed by the prosecution."

The defense teams objected, requesting the release of

their clients. The court upheld the demand of the public prosecutor, denied the requests of the defense, and postponed the hearing.

Outside the courtroom, the magistrate vented his suppressed anger by spitting venom at the officers, who had stopped smiling and bowed their heads.

The postponement was useless. The experts, including the prosecution's, confirmed the previous outcome, and Tonino left the courtroom a free man.

Prior to the trial, a friend of Natalia's had arranged to visit the court-appointed expert, and Santoro's marshal had passed by the crime bureau with a heavy suitcase, replacing the drug with a benign dust.

A large gathering celebrated Tonino's release at one of Milan's most fashionable nightclubs, of which we were part owners. In those days, our happiness still hadn't been overshadowed by the drama.

The work we did had dangerous consequences, but distributing packages didn't get our adrenaline pumping anymore, and it had been a long time since we'd done anything truly exciting. So we were happy when, in October, Sasà took all three of us on one of his trips.

We slipped into one of the many cars that we always kept at the ready and set off toward Northern Europe. We arrived that evening and parked in front of an elegant building in

Munich a few blocks from Marienplatz. The city was celebrating; everyone was drunk. In the very large and vacant
apartment that awaited us, we found four of the boys I'd
met in the Sierra Nevada massif. There were no beds in the
house, so we slept in our sleeping bags, like in the old days
in the mountains.

The following evening, we approached a small border
checkpoint at the end of a bridge over the Rhine that
connected France with Germany. Customs officers hadn't
manned the booth for twenty years, but officially, the border
was still active. The offices were cleaned every morning
and the prominent sign announcing the ten-kilometer-per-
hour speed limit was respected by all those who entered
Germany.

Six of us walked in, each stationing himself by a window.
Luigi and an Arab stayed outside in two separate cars about
fifty feet apart.

The target was an Arab politician who liked to go
around mocking the customs and traditions of his country,
claiming its dictators were enlightened leaders. That was
how Sasà explained it, at least. We weren't concerned with
his motives; a problem for one of us was a problem for us
all, regardless of grievance or reason.

The Arab we intended to kill had held a conference
organized in Strasbourg under the aegis of the European
Community, and would be returning on that road, which
was regarded as more secure.

There would be three victims in total. They were traveling in an armored off-road vehicle. Our cars would cut it off, preventing its escape, and gunfire from six powerful Famas would take care of the armor in no time.

The faint buzzing of two-way radios alerted all eight of us to the target's arrival. Luigi expertly pulled in front of the heavy Range Rover, which was respecting the speed limit, proceeding at the pace of a man on foot. Yussuf closed off the rear. With our six assault rifles, we opened fire on the armored windows, which put up a brief resistance. The bullets breached the cabin and shredded the flesh, bones, and organs of its occupants.

In that deafening din, no one heard the crackle of the two-way radios.

It took us a few seconds to notice that someone was firing on us.

Two men had appeared out of nowhere. We reacted in a flash and riddled the two bodyguards with bullets. But the cost had been steep. Luigi and Yussuf were motionless in their cars. Sasà and one other man had been saved by their bulletproof vests.

The information we'd been given was wrong—the off-road vehicle had not been traveling alone, but was trailed by a spare car.

My heart was in my mouth as we poured out of the customs kiosks. I ran to Luigi, who was stunned. The bullet had hit him in the chest, compressing his thorax. His vest had done its job. He'd only sustained one injury—to his ankle; he was safe.

Yussuf, on the other hand, had a monstrous hole in his left cheek. He was bleeding from his nose and mouth, and the red was flecked with white. He'd been shot point-blank, so the gunpowder had finished combusting on his face, burning his skin and hair. The very short distance didn't allow the projectile to acquire maximum speed and penetration, there was no leakage of brain matter, the wound was not deep, but he was suffocating in his own blood. He opened his eyes and stared at me. He was lost. He didn't want to die, not so far from his desert. He was too young.

We had to decide, and quickly. Leave him there to die and find safety for ourselves immediately, or risk it.

We pulled Yussuf out of the car. We laid him down in the backseat of one of the other two cars we'd brought, and his breathing improved. Luigi joined us without help, hopping on one foot and settling in the passenger seat. I got behind the wheel; the other five got into the second car. We drove a hundred kilometers south and stopped in an empty parking lot. We had to get to Milan to try to save the boy. The shortest way was through Switzerland, and the risk was high.

We took off our weapons and vests, cleaned ourselves up as best we could, and sped off, leaving the three Arabs, who were perfectly able to fend for themselves, even in that situation. Sasà and Luciano drove ahead of us; I followed them with the injured parties.

At the last service area before the border, we bought toll stickers and glued them to our windshields. We crossed the border into Basel, where the customs officers glanced at us only long enough to check for the sticker.

We ran out of luck in Chiasso. The Swiss remained locked in their booths, but four or five Italian customs officers were checking a dozen cars, arranged in two parallel lines.

Sasà lined up in the left row and I by his side, on the right. We had no weapons with us and an escape would have been impossible.

Operations were slow; the military was requesting that the occupants show their documents and open their trunks. There were two cars ahead of us, and I braced myself for the worst. The end of the road. My heart sank.

Improvising, Sasà lowered his window and began to rant in a distorted, drunken voice. He went to step out of the car and the customs officers instantly surrounded him. They motioned to everyone, including me, to keep moving.

They'd taken the bait.

The last I saw of Sasà, he was wriggling as if he'd fallen prey to an epileptic seizure. I arrived in Milan in the middle of the night and tore Natalia out of her bed. She woke the doctor and picked up the phone. A small, fully equipped operating room had been installed in their villa, with an adjoining recovery room.

As he waited for his team, the doctor gave Luigi a painkiller. In less than half an hour, an anesthesiologist, a maxillofacial surgeon, and a specialist nurse had arrived. They took Yussuf inside and emerged four hours later. Then it was Luigi's turn; in twenty minutes, they had applied some sutures and a light cast.

Natalia dismissed the medical team with three checks for one hundred million lire each. I offered to repay her many times, but she never accepted.

After a night in jail, Luciano and Sasà showed up the next day a bit worse for the wear. They'd received a few good kicks and a ticket for resisting arrest and insulting a public official. Or rather, Luciano and Sasà had endured the kicks, but the court summonses would turn out to have been issued to an incredulous Mr. Marzio Ripa, a postal clerk, and an Alfredo Rizzo, a bartender at Milan's central station.

After a few weeks, Yussuf had regained enough strength to leave the small hospital at the villa. Sasà wanted to take him away, but I convinced him to let Yussuf stay a few more days at my place.

I showed him around Milan, loaded him up with presents, took him to the stadium, to the nicest clubs; he'd never been so happy in his life. We all coddled him like a little brother, spending time together at my house, even spending the night.

We boys of the Aurora were like these Arabs, soldiers of an ancient war. The difference was that an entire people shared in their war, while Luciano, Luigi, and I were waging a private battle to no one's benefit but our own. Ultimately, we were risk-takers, and we liked to fight. We couldn't have accepted a normal existence; in the absence of ideals, we would have invented some.

One evening at dinnertime, the national channel broadcast an investigative documentary. The first episode featured an Arab leader who was well known in the West. At the end of the interview, Luigi expressed his unconditional appreciation for the character, in the hopes of pleasing Sasà and Yussuf. "What a legend," he said.

"He's a sell-out," Luciano shot back. "And the favors this country has done for him have brought nothing but grief and pain to Italian mothers."

The room froze for a few seconds.

Sasà laughed. "You must have been born in the Pentagon, Luciano. You always know everything," he said, restoring the lightheartedness that characterized our time together.

That's how Luciano was; in any field, whatever the subject, he'd suddenly declare a searing truth, almost always hard to dispute. He sometimes seemed like the shaman of an ancient tribe, so accurately did he predict the future.

But this time was different; Luciano hadn't come to his own conclusion, and Sasà had caught him. What he knew about this particular man, Luciano had gleaned from the memoirs of Vincenzo Sparta, who knew what was true because he had either heard about it personally or made it happen himself, and not just in matters related to the mafia.

A few days into December, Sasà became adamant about Yussuf's departure. We decided we could close up shop and drove him down to Sicily, weighted down with presents and padded pockets. We watched as he despairingly boarded a fishing boat docked at Porto Empedocle, on his way back to his own country. He couldn't be seen in Europe with that embroidery on his face.

We decided to spend the Christmas holidays in the village, and from Sicily we went directly to my house.

My father had always lived in the same house in the wrinkle. To avoid burying the cash we'd sent him, he'd used it to build another house, a big one, but he never lived in it. That's where the four of us settled, washing up and changing our clothes before going to my parents' for dinner. Only my mother and brother were there. My father and old Bino were still in the mountains, and my five sisters had been living in Rome for years, where they had moved to study and work.

The Aurora had changed; it was nearly empty. We cruised around the village and along the coastal villages, where new houses were being constructed everywhere. A sort of competition had begun for who could build the biggest structure. The wrinkles we'd grown up in had been relegated to the silence of abandonment; they'd become like the shriveled breasts of an old wet nurse. The womb of the Aurora's yellowish barracks would no longer produce life or labor.

The children of the forest rarely missed a holiday in the town of their birth, whether it was Easter, Christmas, or summer vacation. They came back to display their wealth, their beautiful cars; they gave expensive gifts, and brought important friends to show off.

No one tried to hide the nature of his business activities. Despite the sinful origins of the wealth, everyone was happy to enjoy it. Even we weren't immune to that logic. No one could compete with us in either riches or friendships, although we took the precaution not to overdo it. We limited our ostentation so as not to humiliate the proud villagers, since doing so could have proved fatal.

We stayed in the village for a few days, reveling in the respect we'd won, greeting all the returning boys. We sent many of them back to Milan to close pending accounts while we went off into the mountains.

We were shadows in the light. None of us was yet aware of how ridiculous we had become and the disaster we were bringing to our land. Ancient roots that had taken hold a thousand years earlier, defended for centuries, were ripped from the ground and condemned to die. The older generation had reduced itself to parading around in Corneliani suits and Loro Piana cashmere, gold watches and rings. They were parodies of the old shepherds who after years of sweat and emigration hadn't obtained more than a crust of bread for their children, defrauded by pride and the authority of their fathers. The mothers no longer resembled the ones we'd known; they'd loosened their braids, abandoned their traditional clothes; they bought their bread from the baker and had their hair done at the hairdresser's. Sisters and daughters, in garish make-up, sunglasses, and fur coats that were improbable in these warm latitudes, traveled nonstop along the Ionian roads to fulfill who knows what commitments, driving cars with foreign plates sent to them by relatives who walked the streets of Central Europe. Brothers and children dreamed of imitating us one day.

Our ancient world had begun to disappear as soon as our village was transferred from the heart of the Aspromonte to the shores of an Ionian Sea. These celebrations were its funeral, which everyone had mistaken for a party.

The only ones not to rejoice at this happy disaster were the bourgeoisies of old. The peasant masses who had cultivated their land and looked after their beasts, whom the bourgeoisie had exploited and humiliated for centuries, had suddenly been swept out from under their feet. The peasants had attained their own wealth. The former rural masters were now locked in their living rooms, spitting venom and plotting revenge. They sent their children to study law, they enlisted them in law enforcement, they sent them into politics, all in preparation for a comeback. Sooner or later they would put the shackles back on those stinking goatherds and crush their crooked revolt.

When Luciano became possessed by his sociological demon he would say, "We're responsible for the evil we do, we have no alibi, we are our own worst enemies. We can choose how to direct our energy, and we've chosen to take a shortcut to our individual well-being, but if these country dictators hadn't held the reins so tightly for all those centuries, we'd be better behaved and less desperate today. Our local ruling class, with the help of the Blood Brothers, has kept a firm hold on all the wealth. Lawyers are sons of lawyers and nephews of lawyers, and it's the same with judges and doctors. They're better off than we are because they've had more thieving, cunning forebears than we did. They are to blame for everything we children of the forest have done and will continue to do. And now that we don't revere them, we don't ask them for advice, we don't give them the kid goat at Christmas, we don't bring our women into their big beds, and they can't rape them while they work in their fields and homes, they can't stand it, and they're preparing their children for the reconquest, concealing their rancid rage behind their fake ethical principles."

"Those smirking cops," he once commented to me at

one of the Socialist undersecretary's parties. "Tonino's trial was enough to reveal who they really are, sons of bourgeoisie. A poor man would never smile at the pain of others, he knows suffering all too well." Then he gestured to the undersecretary. "Socialists are a little like the children of the forest, they're not elitists, they open their doors to the masses, they look for a piece of heaven and usher in as many people as possible. They love power, but they have the need to flaunt it and they enjoy it with friends. If they manage to get rid of the socialists, that will be the end of us, too, and if we fall, it won't be long until they do."

During that holiday at my father's place, we managed to forget Milan, its dealings, its nonstop pace, and we enjoyed our mountains. Bino came to spend the night with us, leaving my father to return to the Aurora alone. The old goatherd tagged along behind Sasà, in disbelief that he was a foreigner, since he only spoke in our dialect, and with no accent.

Sasà had that gift. He was a chameleon. Looking at him, it was impossible to tell if he was twenty, thirty, or forty years old. I had witnessed him become Spanish, German, Greek, Turkish, Italian, Calabrian. He had an infinite variety of characters that he could adapt according to the environment and his interlocutor. But he had only one, very fixed personality. He was good, happy, of the same breed as Luciano and Sante, and he loved us deeply, there was no faking that.

But Sante, Luciano, and I would have sacrificed everything for our group. We were our own mission. Sasà and Luigi had their limits: one was dedicated to his cause, the other to himself alone.

We spent the long, frigid mountain evenings in front of the hearth inside the house at the fold, with full bellies and a few extra glasses of wine. When a new guest appeared, Bino gave the best of himself, as usual. He would pour some of the local *negrello* and entertain until dawn, telling stories that he swore were true.

One evening he dove right into the story of the Crocco, a famous brigand who wreaked havoc on the foothills the century before.

"Hunger was so widespread here, and inevitably every decade produced its own brigand who terrorized the masters with raids and violence for a few years before he was found hanging from a tree, rotting in the sun or rain, left as a message to potential copycats. That's how it went for Vincenzo Monteleone, a son of this land and its poor peasants who, as a young man, had the unusual idea of feeding himself with his master's beasts. His excessively good health and small paunch, which seemed to appear suddenly, were lost just as quickly. Don Alfonso Barresi, the master, gave him a hard lashing. Then, not yet satisfied, he had the constables escort Vincenzo in chains to the court of Capace, where the presiding judge was the Honorable Don Giovanni Andrea Barresi, the master's cousin and the biggest landowner in the area. The good-natured judge estimated that two years in shackles would be sufficient for Vincenzo's social reform, and that upon his release from jail he would likely take up his hoe and thicken his hands instead of his waistline. His therapy must have been insufficient, however, because once it was over, Vincenzo neglected his hoe in favor of a double-barrel shotgun, and began his life of crime. Once he acquired the necessary arrogance and courage, he went to see Don Alfonso and left him to die in agony, hanging from the crook of a tree, known in dialect as the *crocco*. After the landowner's death, Vincenzo became known far and wide as the Crocco. Destiny had it that Don Alfonso's estate, in the absence of heirs, would supplement the already extensive assets of the Honorable Judge who had sentenced the brigand. Meanwhile the Crocco went unchallenged, ravaging those hungry but very fertile lands for years. It happened eventually that another local gentleman's soul communed with God as he gazed upside down at his beautiful lands, with an ankle firmly lodged in the robust *crocco* of an olive tree. Never having found a partner worthy of him, he too died a bachelor and entirely bereft of heirs. The peasants, who for years had worked that thriving red earth, deluded themselves into thinking that they could claim the estate. But another pack of wolves, more ravenous ones, were preparing to snatch the juicy morsel. Through one of his tenants, Don Giovanni Andrea Barresi secretly contacted the brigand, and coaxed him with promises of certain grace and a generous reward. The Crocco, overestimating his abilities, took the bait. To the tune of gunshots sounding off the mountains, he annihilated the claims of the peasants and forced them to testify in support of the Honorable Judge's petition for the possession of the assets. The judge wanted to personally reward the brigand by arranging a nocturnal meeting at the old convent of Artarusa. The Crocco arrived happy, believing that his times of suffering were over, and looking forward to becoming a gentleman, too, like his illustrious friend. Instead he was met with the constables, who thanked him for his services rendered, and for a month his head remained stuck on a post at a crossroads near the convent. The effective administration of justice always produces excellent results, declared the high magistrate, publicly complimenting the Royal Army, which had freed the people from another bloodthirsty bandit."

The moral of the story, according to old Bino, was that in these lands, both sides had been ruled by brigands for centuries. And so it remained.

"It's all lies, Uncle Bino," Luigi would tease him.

The old man would usually fly into a tizzy, pretending to fall for our provocations, but this time he said to Luigi in a quiet voice, "You bought that diploma of yours." Then he turned to Sasà. "Ask Luciano if you want to know the truth, he's the only one with any brains around here. I don't understand how anyone can spend time with those people. The Barresi family still owns all these lands and runs the court."

Luciano nodded, a gesture that made the old man proud. He didn't hesitate to launch into one of his long-winded speeches, which we'd heard so many times before. He was about to say that there was and would always be a Barresi behind the injustices that suffocated the land, a story I'd grown tired of hearing. I preferred the frost on a starry night and went out to the enclosure to inhale the bitter heather and the breath of the goats, who knew how to live well, with good masters and fragrant grass to eat. They walked along a marked path without a care, and when the end of the journey arrived, it came as the pinch of a compassionate blade that slipped under their necks, carrying away their consciousness and pain and returning their blood to the earth. A quiver of the nostrils and it was over; they found themselves in the eternal prairies of the paradise made by the children of the forest. And if any of them wished to avoid that fate, they could simply cross the river to another pasture, hide on one of the many impossible-to-reach granite peaks, and so long to fences, milking, and knives.

———

A few days before Christmas, Luigi left us to go meet the guests we'd been waiting for. Unexpectedly, a very excited Bino left with him, slipping into my father's old jeep. "I'll see you at the party," he said to Sasà through the open window, and then he and Luigi peeled away.

A dusting of snow appeared from the sky just before nightfall, the air grew magical. Luciano, Sasà, and I attended to the beasts and holed up in the comfortable little house. Our arrangement from years past endured. I stacked the hearth with firewood and made coffee for Luciano, who blissfully smoked a cigarette. Sasà sat near him and together they enjoyed the warmth of the fire.

I began to make dinner. The snow created a surreal silence. I felt alone. I turned to look at them, and only then did I realize something strange. It had been such a long time since they had spoken to each other directly. I understood that both of them wanted to clear the tension that was so contrary to their natures.

I moved the camp stoves outside, arranging everything under the glow of a gas lamp in a small shed recently built by Bino and my father. I let the sauce simmer as I took in the landscape. The snow fell lightly, small dollops of white began to adorn the pines, the placid goats let their newborns greedily suckle at their teats. They were beautiful beasts, nourished and cared for, they had a clean enclosure; their masters were throwbacks from another time and treated them like precious treasures.

For my father and Bino, the concept of time was relative; they accepted very few of the scientific findings that modernity offered and none of its morals. Though they'd endured a period of chaos, they'd overcome it. They lived on what the mountains gave them. My mother wore her braids gathered into a crown, as Bino's wife had done all her life.

Our parents had imposed nothing on us as children, we'd chosen our destinies. After all we'd done, what I most wanted was a life like theirs, and if I'd had the strength to make that change, I know Luciano at least would have followed me. To hell with Milan.

But the world hadn't frightened me enough yet. I shivered, boiled the pasta, and took overflowing plates back into the house. Inside, the storm had passed; they spoke quietly, and I only participated in the last part of their conversation, when they talked about Don Vincenzo Sparta.

Reading Don Vincenzo's memoirs had been an indiscretion, one of the few Luciano had committed in his life. The old boss had poured the misdeeds of a lifetime into his notebooks. Beyond the local woes, he'd detailed an impressive series of offenses in which the Blood Brothers had played a role. Events similar to the one that had brought us to the French border of Germany. His memoirs included names, surnames, and accomplices. After reading them, Luciano understood the danger in knowing such secrets. He hadn't read them out of a vain curiosity; rather he'd been looking for his father's murderer, the one who had armed the late Totò the Blade.

And he'd found him.

Luciano pulled out two small strips of paper and handed them to me. I saw Don Vincenzo's elegant, almost solemn handwriting. There were two short sentences.

Peppino Zacco reported to me on the death of the municipal messenger.

Peppino Zacco reported to me on the death of Sante Motta.

It meant that Zacco had been the one to request consent from the old man for those murders.

While Luciano and Sasà ate peacefully, having vented their anger, my food grew heavy in my mouth.

A suspicion arising from logical deductions is merely a narrative; revenge never leaves you completely satisfied when there is a doubt, however minimal, as to the author of your suffering.

Truth beyond the shadow of a doubt is what grants full vengeance.

The sky gifted us with more snow, and we had a white Christmas. A small parade of cars arrived: my brother and some of my sisters; Giulio, my brother's inseparable friend; Anna, Santoro, and his wife, Chiara, who sweetly attended to him; Rino, the politician, and his wife; Luigi and Natalia.

Bino and my father lingered to greet their own special guest.

That unmistakable gait, that proud chest, that head held high, that man who so long ago had been a swine. It was Leonardo Brambilla and his family.

My thoughts, and those of many, went to Sante. It was an intense period, but like all good things, the holidays flew by, and we grew depressed when the time came for us to return to the North.

THE
BEASTS
IN THEIR
CAGE

No child of the forest was happy about leaving home; we all drove back north slowly, making frequent use of the rest stops. By now, everywhere I went, everyone asked the same thing: "Got any white?"

We'd started hearing the request a few months before; what had first been a lone voice here and there had become a choir.

People weren't seeking out death anymore, or perhaps those who had really wanted to die had done it; now everyone was suddenly infected by the desire to live. And many of them wanted to live incessantly. Demand for the dark stuff diminished in just a few months, prices plummeted, and after a year we found ourselves distributing the last packages at seventeen million lire per kilo. It was the end of an era, and we found ourselves unemployed.

We kept up the good life, frequenting clubs and lounges, and eventually grew bored. The boys, disappointed, gradually stopped seeking us out and started to hound the South Americans. We had no plan for the future, but the demon inside of us was still hungry and drove us forward.

Luciano complained that his brain was rotting; he went back to university and forgot about us. We settled our accounts. Despite our crazy spending and high standard of living, our wealth from those years was still conspicuous.

Through Natalia and her connections, we were able to obtain thousands of bearer savings books at amounts of less than ten million lire each, and scattered them among numerous hiding places at our apartments. We had partnerships in companies and bars, we owned real-estate in every neighborhood. And we had fifty billion lire in cash.

Luigi and Sasà traveled constantly in search of suppliers. Every now and then they would appear, fill a few bags with cash, and leave again. I stayed behind to manage our assets and relationships. I was practically alone, with Luciano intent on finishing his studies, though I would sometimes find a note from him lying around one the apartments we used. That's how we communicated, by letter.

I took up residence in a two-bedroom apartment that we owned on via Eustachi. I hardly went out. In the mornings I'd do the shopping and I spent the evenings with Natalia. Every day I filled my bags with practically useless things at the Esselunga on viale Regina Giovanna. That's where I met Giulia. We ran into each other almost every day with our carts.

We started by exchanging a few fleeting smiles, then moved on to saying hello, and then one morning we found ourselves having breakfast together at the Belle Aurore.

She was a biologist in a testing laboratory. At the time I was going by the name of Antonio De Pierro; I was a medical-scientific representative.

It didn't take long for us to lose ourselves in each other. And my world was driven into crisis.

She was the first normal woman I'd allowed myself to know as a person. With her, I saw a Milan that had been unknown to me until then, a Milan of markets, museums, concerts, mom-and-pop pizzerias, simple people with real problems.

When she finished work, she would meet me at my apartment and we would stay together until the next day. On the weekends, we would travel to nearby attractions outside the city, always something new.

I let her introduce me to her parents, and I began to accept their dinner invitations, often staying to watch television. Sometimes I would fall asleep on their sofa, and Giulia would cover me with a fragrant quilt and wake me in the morning with her mother's coffee.

What was I supposed to do, tell her the truth and hope she understood? Involve her in my life of deceit and violence?

Instead, one evening, I said I would pick her up after work. A light rain was falling, the kind that silences Milan and transforms it into a human, understandable place, relieving the weight of the air. I arrived early and parked some distance from the door. I saw her walk out. She clutched her light gray raincoat tightly against her. She lifted the brim of her curious Panama hat to look down the road, anticipating my arrival. She was a happy woman. Every man's dream. My dream.

I started the engine and disappeared from her life. The relationship was forcing me to reflect, something I couldn't allow myself to do.

I escaped to save her. That was my excuse; my whole existence had been a pile of fucking excuses. Until then, I'd divided women into saints and whores, but she was not a doll to be placed on an altar or slammed against a mattress. She was a normal person, the world was full of them, even if it had felt safer for me to divide it into friends and enemies. And normal people are not figurines that you can arrange as you like. When I was a child, my father would sometimes lose his temper in response to that serious, worried look I often had on my face. "What have you got in that head of yours?" he'd cry. I didn't have one shit inside my head, just a monster that devoured me. A bloody clot of evil. I should have run away from my father, from the others, then maybe I would have happily become a shepherd. Luciano would have ended up in a laboratory inventing something useful, maybe Sante would have stopped coming back to kill people, and Santoro would have grown fond of his uniform over time. I'd always invented a cause to fight for in order to keep others close to me. In fact, though, I was a prisoner of my fears, a vessel for the worst of a cultural network that was losing its significance. I was out of my mind, and perhaps no one even noticed. I'd tried to slay the monster inside me, but it was a big black bull with a shiny, silken coat, and a lead bullet hadn't been enough to bring it down. Luciano had been right about one thing, which was that we, children of the forest, were part beast, only harmless when caged in our mountains.

I went to spend the night in the apartment on via Savona and found Santoro dozing in the bed, waiting for me. "Tonino found them," he said.

For years, we'd been hunting two of the surviving assassins sent by Zacco to kill Sante. We couldn't risk an outright war with Don Peppino; he was too powerful. After Vincenzo Sparta's death, Don Peppino had taken his place, and we risked finding ourselves up against an entire army of Blood Brothers. Instead, we led a covert war, imitating the strategy of those saint-burners: officially we were friends with them and had no notion that Zacco had anything to do with Sante's death.

We were aiming to weaken Zacco gradually. Every so often we would eliminate some of his most dangerous minions. If questioned, we swore we knew nothing about it. In that world of tragedies it was difficult to identify who was to blame; what an enormous burden, trying to figure out who, among so many enemies, most deserved a hit.

Death sentences were always issued with doubt.

Tonino had found the assassins in Genoa; they were getting weed from one of his men. We sent the marshal to study their movements, and after a week of tracking them he discovered where they lived. We woke them at dawn wearing Benemérita uniforms and driving a police car. They came with us peacefully in handcuffs, knowing the routine. They only started kicking when they noticed we were driving into the open countryside instead of into Marassi. They disappeared into nothingness, and Genoa was freed from their stench.

After that hit, Santoro quietly dedicated himself to his newborn little Sante. Luigi and Sasà reappeared to ask me to go in on a trucking company with them, with a few tractor trailers traveling to Spain on a weekly basis. Luciano also reappeared, in good spirits, and invited us all to dinner, announcing that there would be a special guest. The end of my relationship with Giulia had brought me back to my version of normalcy, with its unshakable certainties. My serious disposition allowed me to keep believing that I was a genius.

For his dinner, Luciano had chosen the Botte on via Ripamonti. Tonino, Santoro, the marshal, Rino, Natalia and I had already taken our seats when Luciano arrived. I couldn't believe my eyes when he walked in with Stefano

Bennaco, the jocular fugitive who had sought refuge in my father's mountain hideout so many years ago before escaping to Basque Country. Rino told us everything. They'd been working on it for a long time, engaging legal luminaries, renowned experts, offering them bulging envelopes. Eventually they'd gotten Stefano's sentence repealed. After many long years in hiding, his life imprisonment sentence for a kidnapping gone wrong was no longer hanging over his head.

Stefano celebrated with us, and we took him and the family he had formed in Spain on a weeklong tour of Milan. Then he left for Calabria to introduce his mother to the grandchildren she'd never met. Luciano was like that; what he got in his head to do he did without being asked. He worked slowly but always hit the mark. We'd spent happy days with Stefano when he was a "shadow" hiding in our fold. He had never forgotten our hospitality. He had always sent gifts from Spain to us or to my father. Now, Luciano had happily repaid him for his loyalty and affection.

Eventually, the travels of Luigi and Sasà and all the money they spent bore fruit, and they returned with definitive proposals. Luciano, Santoro, the marshal, Tonino—now a permanent member of the group—and I gathered at Natalia's villa. She let us have the place to ourselves and went out on the town with her distinguished husband.

Sasà had learned all about cocaine and proved it. Cocaine

had been around for years, for all of time, one might argue. Almost everyone kept it at an arm's length because it was a restricted market, it cost too much and few could afford it. Everyone thought it was Colombian, but it was mainly produced in Bolivia, on the border with Brazil. Colombians were the major traffickers, and sold ninety percent of the product in North America. That was the biggest market in the world; cocaine was mass-consumed there, for a very simple reason: the only currency the South Americans would accept was the dollar. They demanded $35,000 a package and transported it by land. Hundreds of millions of people were able to spend fifty dollars for a gram, almost pure. Each shipment amounted to several tons of product. But an Italian buyer first had to change lire for dollars, and spend seventy million lire to get $35,000. You had to import it yourself, because the big traffickers wouldn't bother for transports of less than three or four tons, and the little traffickers couldn't handle it. So after you bought it, you also had to move it, which meant at least a thousand dollars a package to load it, a thousand to ship it by cargo, another thousand to unload it, and a thousand for ground transport. In order to make a decent profit, you had to sell it at around ninety million lire per package on a first-hand delivery; retail came to one hundred and twenty million. In Western Europe, few could afford to traffic on those terms, and it was no surprise that cocaine was a rich man's drug. The supposed "white" that was floating around was almost always a synthetic drug prepared in some Dutch laboratory or, as Santoro explained, since he often saw the test results for narcotics seized by the Carabinieri, a mix of cutting substances: lidocaine, boric acid, plus ether for an anesthetic effect and amphetamines to act as a stimulant. In that mixture, coca alkaloid was present at less than ten percent, sometimes even less than five. That was the only way to bring the price down to around fifty thousand lire per gram, which the masses could afford, at least on occasion.

Sasà said that all of his contacts with the Colombians had failed, that they didn't consider the European market to be desirable at the moment. But with Luigi he'd been able to get further. In Bolivia the growing was done in broad daylight, and it wasn't hard to find suppliers. The crop was sometimes so abundant that the leaves were left to rot on the ground. They could buy it for five hundred dollars a pound, and they'd already connected with wholesalers. The local relationships had been secured, as had ground transport to the Brazilian ports, and transport by sea to Spain. We would take care of the last leg to Italy with our trucks, which were already shuttling toward Barcelona.

All we were missing were a couple of everyday chemicals and the products needed for refinement. Natalia procured the materials and personnel, whom we brought to Spain. Luigi and Sasà went with them. To set the entire mechanism into motion required economic savvy, knowledge of means, people, places, and guarantors, which at that moment only we possessed.

Of course, Sasà and Luigi took all the credit. Luciano, who had a passion for politics at that time, said this scheme would destroy us, and he disappeared again.

We created a market in Milan and kept a firm grip on it for years. Once the prices went down, we got the attention of the Colombians, who monopolized sales in Northern Europe. Italy was the richest European market, especially Milan. We managed to produce a finished product at a cost of about twenty million lire. Then we flipped it to the Calabrians at twenty-eight or thirty million per package.

We were back on our path. Everyone was seeking us out again and I can't deny that we loved it. Even Luciano couldn't resist it, and to everyone's joy he returned to oversee the accounting. We had stepped into the nineties, and the new decade was proving itself to be richer and happier than the one before it. The new criminal procedure code had made its debut, bringing with it amnesty and pardons; from now on, trials would be conducted the American way, on equal grounds between the prosecution and defense. There was a widespread sense that the state had assumed a strategy of tolerance, and even heavy sentences were mitigated by a general application of the Gozzini law, which governed the lives of prisoners.

Everyone wanted to get straight and emerge from the shadows. The children of the forest relaxed their defenses and started to own assets and companies under their own names; they drove around in their luxurious cars with their real driver's licenses. They believed they would be accepted, finally, as legitimate Italians, the children of a noble nation.

Then came the summer of the World Cup, with its magical nights. We went out en masse to cheer for Italy. Everyone thought the honeymoon had been extended.

But it was over. We lost the World Cup. That fall, little attention was paid to the issuance of Presidential Decree 309/90, the new law on drugs, and the changes that began to undermine the guarantee mechanism of the new legal code.

Luciano was among the very few to keep his guard up. He explained that aggravated penalties for drug dealers were expanding dramatically, and alternative processes could now be implemented to obtain an easy confession from the defendant and a guilty verdict. No one yet understood the lethal trap presented by wiretapping and its admission as evidence in a trial. The old regime was trying to save itself with those new laws. Few sensed the imminent collapse of a power system that had gripped the nation for half a century.

Luciano forced us to adhere to the precautions we'd adopted in the eighties. He preached his warnings to others, but he was speaking to the wind. He also put Rino and his friends on notice; he'd been familiarizing himself with certain political circles and the educated and moralistic world that fueled them. Even in roaring Milan, where most people were determined to enjoy the good life, there were, he said, powerful groups that swelled with horror at the thought of the burgeoning drug trade. They couldn't bear to go to restaurants, stadiums, concerts, and be relegated to waiting behind stinking peasants and shepherds who had grown rich from their delinquency, or to watch the ascent of arrogant and ignorant politicians who were in league with the former. The so-called cultured classes, imbued with moralism and in union with political circles eager to seize power in short order, were ready to launch their offensive.

But there was a general lack of suspicion about the coming storm, a widespread headiness, a sense of omnipotence and, of course, an intolerable arrogance. No one bothered to consider the evidence.

Rino repeated Luciano's warning to his friends, yet his words were drowned out by their laughter; the people were with them, they said; they were making ordinary people feel more at home than ever in the Republic. They felt untouchable.

Undaunted, we continued to grind coke and make billions. We received thousands of packages that gave off a sweet, caramelized scent of peaches and violets. The white, unlike the dark, did not inspire fear. When we opened it, the crystals burst with elation, tufts of aromatic talc rose up, and it immediately dissolved between our fingertips, leaving behind a light, oily patina. The dark stuff stank of something wild, the stench of a beast, of poisonous oleander; it was difficult to get rid of, it was a dirty brown color, and it had to be melted with fire. With heroin you immediately saw blood, and it was intimidating. Coke adhered peacefully to the nasal mucosa, it seemed harmless, and left no marks on the body.

The children of the forest carried on, living like birds of prey in Milan, a paradigm of Western Europe. In the beginning, they had been aware that they were foreigners in this northern land, and they respected their surroundings. They had known that their wealth was stolen, and therefore they shared it. Now, though, they had convinced themselves that the money was all theirs, and they began to behave badly, all-powerfully. When they emerged from the shadows, they revealed the evil they carried in their bodies, and showed the worst of themselves. The enchantment of our Italian honeymoon was marred by their dark shadows.

The new drug had lost the momentum of its early years, and fun became diseased, a thing of the past. Instead of selling cocaine, the boys began to use it. They dealt just enough to cover their personal vices. They started arriving late for meetings and then forgot about them entirely. In order to meet someone, you had to get him out of bed, or wait for nighttime. They all lived from dusk to dawn.

It was no fun spending time with the children of the forest anymore. They nonchalantly recounted their incredible hallucinations, they saw cops everywhere and traitors in their best friends. They began to shoot at each other over imagined slights, and when they pulled out their guns they were often so baked that innocent bystanders suffered the worst.

We started to dislike the game more and more.

We weeded out our less reliable customers, restricting the circle of dealers we worked with, or their number of visits.

It was around that time when a strange bacterium suddenly started to spread around Milan, causing attacks of dysentery and manifesting itself in hundreds of red dots on faces and chests. At the bars where we met our customers we could barely finish a conversation, and the lines for the bathrooms were substantial. With a smile on his lips, Luciano recited the names of every plague. Only we and a few other boys seemed to be immune to the disease.

When the bacterium had been dominating the city for over a week, we all went out to dinner together. I laughed when Luigi and Sasà arrived, their faces burning like infants with rubella. Tonino and Luciano grew livid, and launched into a malicious rant against them. There was a tension between us that had never existed before. Then I understood why.

"If you start using," said Luciano, "we're finished." The marshal, Santoro, and I made a concerted effort to restore calm at the table and understand what had happened: it had been Tonino's idea, but only Luciano's scientific knowledge had made the practical joke possible.

The fact that almost everyone who dealt coke also used it was apparent from their change in character, habits, punctuality, and precision. Of course, everyone denied the obvious, and belittled other users.

"You know like they do with robberies, when they fill bags of money with paint and let them burst all over the thieves' faces? What if we could color the users' faces the same way? We'd shame them all," Tonino had commented to Luciano as they waited for a no-show customer in Piazzale Lodi. Liking the suggestion, Luciano opened a discreet number of packages and sprinkled a bacterium inside, the effects of which only lasted a few days. He resealed everything and took up a pen and paper, noting which of our business contacts showed up with the mark of vice.

Sasà and Luigi swore up and down they had never touched the stuff, and offered an explanation: they claimed they'd realized a package had been opened and closed badly and cut it open to check its contents. When they did, the package broke and its contents dispersed in a cloud over the table. That must have been why they'd inhaled the stuff by accident. Now their backsides were in flames from the constant wiping, all because of those two ballbreakers, Luciano and Tonino.

We wanted to believe it was true; after all, I'd also felt lightheaded sometimes after opening packages to check them. Still, as of that day, a malignance insinuated its way into our union.

The joke was out, and for some time people suddenly had to leave Milan for work. Customers started to observe the effects of the drug on other people before inhaling any white that came from us.

To put the spat behind us, Sasà took us with him to Paris.

We were still allocating a large part of our earnings to his Arab friends; we'd gotten our start thanks to them and it seemed right to go on like this.

Sasà was en route to Paris to handle an arms supply. We arrived at the Charles de Gaulle International Airport dressed like businessmen and took two taxis to Avenue Montaigne; we checked into two splendid suites at the Plaza Athénée, next to the princely love nest of a well-known Lebanese businessman, who closed the deal with Sasà over an animated dispute. While the two of them argued, we ate voraciously and stripped the beautiful Moor waitresses with our eyes. When the two stopped arguing and shook hands, the Lebanese man left us to have our way with his attendants.

The next day we played tourist, exploring Paris with our cameras—the Champs Élysées, Place Vendôme, Place de la Concorde, Les Invalides, the Louvre, the Trocadéro. In the evening, already a little tipsy, we concluded our holiday in a nightclub on George V. It took us some time to notice that the waitresses and all the women on stage were transvestites. Only men occupied the other tables, and they eyed us lustfully. By the time we realized, it was too late to stop Tonino.

We jokingly called him Tonino, a little boy's nickname, but his real nickname was the Doberman. Nearly six foot five, he had to be kept on a short leash, because he would go on the attack if he thought other people found him ridiculous, and it was always a disaster.

After Tonino flipped the first two tables, the queens reacted quickly. A hoard of them came at us, and we fended off a few before eventually succumbing. It was a massacre, but the worst was yet to come, when the fearsome metropolitan police, the *flics*, arrived in their black jackets and took all of us to the station opposite Concorde-Lafayette and tortured us until dawn. Then they issued us expulsion orders for being undesirables and loaded us into a big Peugeot van. We passed through airport customs and boarded an Air France flight to Rome-Fiumicino. Once we landed, we were booked and released.

We laughed for months imagining the faces of the Frenchmen's wives when they heard that their husbands, whose advances we'd warded off, had spent a night in jail for a brawl in a men's only establishment in downtown Paris.

It wasn't funny to everyone; back in Milan, unsuspecting French tourists who came within earshot of Tonino and made the mistake of answering his distorted question of *"Vu sette franses?"* with a *"oui"* found themselves facing down an angry bull. For months, peaceful transalpine citizens filed complaints of inexplicable assaults with the service inspector at the San Sepolcro Commissariat.

That trip put things right between us. But our work became increasingly difficult as people like us became the cops' main focus. Not a day passed without a raid that led to the arrest of dozens. Increasingly stringent legislation and modern technologies rendered the children of the forest—no longer predators as much as they were puppets—easy prey to repression.

Everyone was working on the go. The boys had three or four cell phones each; the phones had appeared some years earlier with the false assurance that calls couldn't be tapped, so everyone spoke freely, scheduling meetings that the law also managed to attend. Between telephone records and fuzzy conversations picked up by the bugs installed in our vehicles, the cops had enough evidence to hold up any charges that might be filed.

The right-minded folk had suddenly awakened, as if they hadn't been feasting with us for years; they demanded and obtained increasingly harsher anti-drug laws. We were a cancer, according to public opinion, and we must be eradicated.

Newspaper and TV narratives advocated for an erosion of the legal defense guarantees established by the laws of the former regime. From the prisons, bosses ordered their people on the outside to lay low, but there was no preventing panic and deaths mounted all over Italy. Under the circumstances, we should have all done our best to lead quiet, uneventful lives, and yet strangely, people committed senseless acts of violence that drew attention to themselves instead. Acts that would lead to our demise.

Our group's way of operating, the way we covered

ourselves, had spared us from the carnage of daily arrests. We had never used landlines, let alone cell phones. When the bugs started to appear, we went out into the open countryside to discuss work; we no longer frequented the bars, and before making any new moves, we would disappear completely from circulation.

We lived more and more of our lives in the shadows.

Santoro, who had become a captain in the force, continuously provided us with lists of informants and ongoing investigations. Our friends in other police departments did the same for a fee.

But it was a game of cat-and-mouse, and only the deluded could have believed they would win against the means and men of the state, which had decided to wipe us out.

The countdown had begun, and the only difference between us was how long each would last. The people on our heels could waste all the time they wanted, their paychecks would arrive at the end of the month just the same, they had an easy job, they were protected, they had nothing to lose. Their mistakes had no serious consequences, while a slip-up on our part could mean thirty years in prison.

Our group was luckier than the others; we had friendships, an ocean of money; we were well-versed in how the cops worked, where they placed the bugs, how they made their preliminary identifications, their random checks, the type of cameras they affixed to the lampposts. All we had to do was cut the cord and leave them empty-handed.

But in order to interrupt the mechanism that granted us so much wealth and power, we would have needed the kind of willpower that only Luciano still possessed. We made sure to stamp any such determination out of him. We didn't give it all up; on the contrary, we grew increasingly bitter toward our enemies.

One day Sasà announced he had to take care of something that he "couldn't get out of," as he put it, his eyes downcast. And so we prepared for a new journey. We were caught up in an operation whose ramifications we pretended not to understand, but on which our past had depended and our future would be decided.

A Bulgarian agent and defector had found refuge in an embassy on via Veneto in Rome. For decades, he had acted as the link between Italian informants and the higher-ups at his agency behind the curtain. He had information on thirty years of misdeeds in our beautiful country, and now he was spilling everything. It would have caused an earthquake in certain political circles and destroyed several budding projects.

Our alibis ended there. In truth, our game was transparent, and we could no longer pretend that we didn't understand. But Sasà begged us not to ask questions; he said we had to trust him. It was essential to our salvation.

The marshal procured two military police cars and we left for Rome. In addition to the cars, Sasà had requested a colonel's uniform. At the mouth of via Veneto, we activated our sirens and flashing lights and got out of the cars in front of the embassy, leaving the doors open. Our very own Colonel Arenghi, a supposed member of the anti-terrorism squad, ordered our colleagues standing guard at the site to follow us inside: there had been a very reliable bomb threat, and we had to carry out a preliminary check before the alerted bomb squad intervened.

We knew all the procedures, and no one was alarmed. The embassy's internal security officers unsuspectingly accompanied the colonel, who carefully explained the details of the operations in perfect English. After we inspected the offices, the colonel entered the Bulgarian ambassador's private quarters—alone, in the name of discretion—while I stood by the half-closed door. When I heard a slight commotion, I rushed in. Sasà had already taken care of his target and his escort, and was holding a small 22mm to the forehead of the diplomat, whom he proceeded to immobilize.

We calmly left; it had been a false alarm. Our colleagues returned to their posts, and the colonel relieved them of their reporting duties, insisting that he would personally send a note to his department.

We returned to Milan without incident. News of the event didn't appear that day or in the days thereafter. It had all been a dream. Very real, on the other hand, were the cutting words that Luciano shouted at Sasà and Luigi as he drove us home. They were in the back, while I was in the passenger seat next to Luciano.

He stopped the car at a service area, turned around, and laid into them, pouring out everything he had been keeping inside for years. He addressed Luigi first: "Do you have anything in that fucking head of yours besides money? Do you have any feelings? A single passion? Do you think about anything besides business? We've been attached at the hip for a lifetime and I've never seen a single tear in your eye. You wouldn't even cry over our dead bodies, you'd just kneel to take our wallets." Then he turned to Sasà: "Do you think you're the only one with a people, a cause? Our people are progeny of a warrior lineage. Greeks, Romans, Arabs, Spaniards, they all tried to take the Aspromonte and never made it past the foothills. No empire has ever conquered the children of the forest. This was the last of the dirty work we'll ever do for your friends. We aren't tin soldiers, and we're not taking orders from anyone. Tell them we're our own masters and let them do whatever the fuck they want about it." No one opened his mouth again for the rest of the trip.

Our world was crumbling fast.

Dealers and gangsters began to clear their consciences, mostly by confessing the sins of others. At first there were only a few rats, but a mass desertion soon followed.

We already had a list of names of the first informants to roll—or "repent." Denunciations that had been kept in the dark for years were now forced into the light of day before the prosecutors. The informants had to be sworn in at the courtrooms, with their backs to the full defendant's cages.

It was a bloodbath. At first, while Sicilian and Campanian mafiosi decimated their own ranks, taking out the rats and trying to short-circuit the arrests, the children of the forest held out; their families would have disowned any traitors. But they were weakened by too many vices, and eventually the defections began.

The truly repentant informants would sign anything; the more self-serving never shared everything they knew, and they never told the unadulterated truth, but would begin by ruining their personal enemies, making them out to be more important than they were, attributing all misdeeds to those already serving jail sentences, and in reality sacrificing very few of their own friends.

There were thousands of arrests. Those people destroyed our world. It wasn't the incarcerations; our lands could immediately replace fathers with their children, children with grandchildren. But the real blow to our culture was psychological. No one trusted anyone, nor would they ever again. The army of predators that had marched the streets of Western Europe was disintegrating.

People like us were replaced by new depraved souls: Slavs, Albanians, Arabs, South Americans, Africans. Milan would never benefit from the revolution that took us down; it simply exchanged one criminal system for another. We were no saints but, paradoxically, we had represented minor danger for ordinary people. In our own way, we knew the moral codes, and when we violated them we did so mindfully. The new arrivals brought violence, bitterness, and blind, indiscriminate destruction. We were no better than they were, but at least when we were around, people hadn't been afraid to go out; later, they were. Cash disappeared from circulation.

The avengers of the new regime, some in good faith and others less so, were wiping us out as they cleaned house. They were reducing Milan to a shadow of itself, and the people applauded. On the streets, criminals began to rape, bag-snatch, rob, and kill over nothing. The people, locked in their homes, watched thousands of children of the forest being led away in handcuffs, powerful politicians sweating and mumbling before the new courts, and they enjoyed the show.

We had certainly been evil, and we deserved to be punished. But justice made nothing better; even without people like us on the streets, the world failed to improve.

Drug dealers were doing real jail time now, while on the outside people complained that the criminals got off too easily. Nonsense. Pedophiles, rapists, thieves, pick-pockets, assassins and contract killers who took out mafiosi, politicians and poor, hungry migrants, would be released after a few days on the inside to go back to their important responsibilities to the Milanese. However, if your crime was included among those under Article 4b, if you were associated with mafia organizations or drug traffickers, you did real prison time, and it was hard time. You could forget about a reduced sentence.

It was only fair that they made us pay, but in the end it was only people like us who did time.

Not us, personally. In the eye of the storm, our group was grinding coke and making billions, undaunted and unscathed. It seemed as though the cops and informants had forgotten our names.

But Natalia's living room had grown deserted; there were only a few of us left. It was at one of these survivors' meetings that Rino passed me a typescript. "My friends thank you," he said, "but there won't be a need for this, the storm will pass, everything will work itself out." I read the document later; it was in Luciano's style. Only he would have been able to produce such a thing. It was a dossier, the first part of which described the vices, virtues, addresses, friendships, and habits of very famous people, as well as those of others who were perfectly unknown to me. According to Luciano, these were the main culprits of the current judicial revolution. The second part laid out a plan for their physical elimination, which would take place through the creation of a fictional subversive group, which Luciano had named the LAL, the Liberation Army of Locri, whose declared purpose was the autonomy of our region of origin and the liberation of all the prisoners born there. The true purpose of the organization, through multi-pronged attacks, was to kill the enemy targets.

The plan might have seemed impossible, but at that time we were in a position to implement it, or at least try. We could get hundreds of guys involved; we had the money, the weapons, and the lack of conscience required to pull it off.

I passed along the news to Luciano that Rino and his friends had refused the offer and returned the dossier. "With everything they did for us, we owe it to them," he told me. "Call the others, we have to talk," he said as he left.

All of us attended Luciano's meeting, including Natalia. He spoke at length: "The three of us started off as desperate goatherds and rose up to challenge the Blood Brothers and the cops. Then Sante joined us, opening our eyes to many things and defending us to the death. In Milan, we met Sasà, who helped us arrive at unimaginable riches. We reunited with Santoro, and it was as if Sante were with us again. Natalia rejoined us. And then there was Tonino, Alfio, and other friends. United, we've traveled dangerous roads together, and we've achieved everything we set out to do and more. Now, the sun is setting on this world we've created. We belong, perhaps without knowing it, to an age that has already passed. Milan gave us so much, and took something from us, from inside of us. We live lives that are not our own, with people we no longer like, we operate on autopilot, waiting to crash. We have become the extras, not the protagonists, of a play directed by others. We'll end up in a ditch or rotting in jail, with Don Peppino Zacco laughing at us. We'll meet some fucking Albanian who will put six inches of steel in our stomachs. It's just a matter of time. Still, apart from the tragedy of what happened to Sante so long ago, everything has gone all too well. We are, as they say, young and rich. We can still go out on top."

Luciano paused to let his speech seep into our consciences. Then, knowing that he had to give Luigi and Sasà an extra push to convince them, he made a proposal. We would organize one last run—a huge one. We would sell all our remaining merchandise exclusively to the four or five larger groups that used us. He and Natalia would monetize the company shares, houses, and all the assets we held. Then they would move all our liquid assets into foreign bank accounts. In the meantime, Tonino would transport about ten billion lire and a decent supply of weapons to the South, storing it in the remote mountains of our countryside, where Stefano Bennaco and the four or five other interrelated families were living.

Once we organized the money and coke, we would finally close accounts with Zacco. After that, those who wished could follow us into whatever our next endeavor would be, or they could take their share of the money and do whatever they pleased.

We all welcomed the plan; it was liberating, and we were tired. Having a concrete goal gave us the motivation we needed to go on. Implementation would be difficult but not impossible. It was the right dream for the moment, and we felt united again after so much time swallowing our feelings.

We threw ourselves headlong into the operation; Sasà and Luigi organized a five-ton shipment. We contacted the major downtown traffickers and got them involved, making them pay a share of the costs of the trip up front. As soon as it arrived, the coke was delivered in huge quantities to the new members, who quickly got themselves out of the red. Santoro and Alfio transported our constant cash flow to Lugano, Switzerland, where Natalia and Luciano distributed it among our accounts, which had been opened in Brazil. Tonino threw himself into his assignment, traveling up and down the country by car. My brother, Gino, and his friends, Giulio and Ciccio, lent a hand.

We worked without pause for a few months. When just a few coins remained to be collected, we relaxed. Of all the real estate we'd held, we'd only kept a two-room apartment in via Spartaco, just behind the courthouse, where we stayed in anticipation of our departure in the coming days. We abandoned our usual precautions—no more weapons or false documents. We bought a small car for our trip in my name, since traveling no longer posed a risk.

We were in the habit of getting up just before noon, having breakfast at the Tre Marie on via Bergamo, taking a spin to get our appetites up, then heading to a small tavern in the Barona area, frequented only by sales representatives. One Friday morning, we finally decided that we were done.

After the meeting we had planned for that afternoon, we would shut ourselves in the apartment until our departure the next day, destination Calabria.

We were ready for the best part.

But the best part came for us first.

After our usual breakfast, we got in the car, which I was driving. I first noticed them a few cars behind ours when we were in the thick of traffic on viale Liguria. That malicious smile was unmistakable. Years had passed, but the smirk was the same: it belonged to the cop who had thrown Tonino his party, which we had spoiled by replacing the evidence.

I relaxed. We had nothing to fear, we were clean, and maybe it was a coincidence. I pulled out of our lane as if to find a clearer route, and the cops turned with us. It wasn't a coincidence. They seemed too pleased with themselves, and my temples began to buzz as I slipped down narrow streets in the direction of the tavern. I told the others to get out of the car one at a time when I braked, and not to ask any questions.

There was no room for Luciano to open his door, but Luigi jumped out fast and disappeared down an alley. Then it was Sasà's turn. He was quick, too, but not like Luigi. We were at the end of via Binda when I tried again with Luciano. He just managed to crack open the door. When he did, he was met by the barrel of a Beretta 92SF 9x21 caliber against his forehead and froze. Two cars in front of us and two behind forced us to surrender. The peace was over.

They opened the trunk and pulled out a heavy black duffel bag. They probably had an orgasm when twenty packages spilled out. I'd never seen the bag before, but I didn't need a clairvoyant to know what had been planted on us. I'd handled packages like those thousands of times.

They handcuffed us. A small crowd formed around us, applauded contentedly, hurled insults; someone called us peddlers of death. "Maybe you'll all live better now," I shouted back.

Sirens accompanied us all the way to the Fatebenefratelli. The cops had their fun making a mockery of us. We didn't take it personally, we understood them, we knew what revenge was, and that the victors were entitled to savor it.

They thrust our ink-stained fingers onto cards printed with our faces and names, then unloaded us at a prison just outside Milan. They would go home to their small houses, their families, and in a few days we would be nothing more than a memory for them; we were work, not people. They were unaware, perhaps, of the drama their revenge would cause.

The correction officers stripped us, booked us, confiscated our belongings, and led us, trousers in hand, to the solitary confinement block, where they placed us in two separate cells, per the magistrate's orders.

We signed our names in the register and designated our legal representation, a renowned lawyer who was a longtime friend of ours. After a few days, we were led by our leashes, steel chain sheathed in black plastic, to the preliminary investigations judge. In the place of the luminary we had chosen as our representative, we were met by one of his young partners, apologizing that his colleague was bedridden with the flu. That was when we understood how powerful our enemies were, and how serious our predicament.

We availed ourselves of the right to remain silent. The judge issued a precautionary detainment order against us. Our attorney appealed to the review court. We took another journey on our leashes. The hearing lasted a few minutes, enough time for us to declare our innocence and explain that we'd been framed. The presiding judge smiled good-naturedly and issued his ruling, which was communicated to us in short order: our petition was rejected and we were sentenced to pay all court fees, in the amount of one million lire.

After a week, we were formally removed from solitary confinement, but since the high-security block was overcrowded we were stuck there almost a month waiting for space.

Anguish consumed us. We leapt up from our cots at the slightest sound. The officer in charge of the mail walked straight past our cells; he had asked us for money, but we didn't have a single lira on prison credit. We couldn't buy anything, no newspapers, no cigarettes for Luciano.

For two hours each day we were released into a ten-by-thirteen-foot pen that they called fresh air. We thought up a thousand scenarios about who could have framed us. It wasn't prison that tormented us as much as the fact that a month had passed without anyone coming to visit. We knew very well that it was the silence of death.

How many, we wondered. And who.

Then one night, they made us gather our things and led us to the high-security block, cell number seventeen. Our legs refused to move; the officer had to shout to get us to budge.

Inside, we found that some Blood Brother had arranged a welcome for us: a stack of newspapers on the top bunk.

Luciano had no one on the outside, so he was the one to read. I lay on the lower bunk, closed my eyes, and waited. I could hear the pages turning. The rest of the block was silent. They respected our grief.

Finally, Luciano recited the list: Santoro, Alfio, Natalia, Bino, my father. Tonino was in critical condition.

I sunk into a deep sleep, my only defense against the crushing annihilation. Luciano suffered as much as I did, but in a different way. The pain that had been doled out to my mother, my sisters, my brother, to Anna, to Chiara, to Alfio's family, was entirely of my own making.

I thought about us as kids, those first heists we'd pulled off so we could dress better at school. Luigi would greedily count the spoils, while Luciano, in his imploring, even prophetic tone, would say, "Let's stop while we're ahead." But I was the one who drove us forward, and now a river of hatred coursed through my body, sweeping up everyone in its path, though the person I most detested was myself.

Even though he was more broken by what had happened than I was, Luciano acted like my nurse. He never left me alone, telling me the same story a thousand times.

After more than a month, they called me to visitation hours. Luciano shaved me, forced me into the shower, and made me put on clean clothes. "You're everyone's rock," he told me, "you have to keep your head up."

My brother had come alone. That surprised me. He was reactive, maybe too much; his hatred exceeded his pain, and he wanted to destroy the world.

I talked to him quietly, calmed him down, and asked him to walk me through everything that had happened. After our arrest, Sasà and Luigi had disappeared from circulation and hadn't been heard from again. Santoro and Alfio had been driving on the west ring road when their police car was overturned by a heavy truck whose driver had fallen asleep at the wheel. Natalia was found dead from a massive overdose of tranquilizers. Our old men had been slaughtered while opening the gate to my father's own goat fold; he and Bino hadn't wanted to leave their animals penned up when they went into hiding at Stefano's, as Santoro and Alfio had recommended. The assassins had desecrated their bodies, completely disfiguring poor Bino, who was almost a hundred years old; a flutter of wings would have been enough to take him down. This time, no one could have held back the Doberman, Tonino, who escaped Stefano's restraint in the dead of night to search for the old men after they'd failed to show up. The assassins were waiting for him, and unloaded their rifles into his chest before they fled, assuming they'd killed him. Marshal Palamita loaded Tonino into his jeep and took him to the hospital; the barrier of muscle he had in place of a human chest had taken all the bullets, shielding his organs. His recovery had been slow.

Almost no one had attended the old men's funerals; only the Aurora, and some of the elders who lived in the countryside, plus a couple of boys for whom gratitude was stronger than fear. But Leonardo Brambilla had gone down to mourn his friends and comfort their relatives. He stayed for a week, trying, in vain, to get my brother to come back up with him when he left.

Don Peppino had made an appearance, too, and in good company, to offer his condolences. He patted my brother's shoulder and said, "You can put your hearts to rest, tell your brother and Luciano I'm through."

Our visiting time was up. Giulio and Ciccio were waiting for my brother outside.

I rejected my brother's proposals for revenge and told him that as long as I was alive, I would be the one to make the decisions.

"Go stay with Stefano, all of you. We won't be cooling our heels in here for much longer." I smiled, adding that he didn't need to visit often, once every four or five months would do, as long as he kept our accounts topped up.

He left, relieved of the responsibilities he'd thought he would have to take on.

Luciano and I spent our two hours in the courtyard for "air" everyday. We knew at least half of our fellow prisoners, though they could barely muster a greeting when they saw us and insisted on keeping their distance. So many of them had rubbed elbows with us when times were good. We'd given each of them something: a job, advice, a hookup with our influential friends during a legal dispute. But that was in the past now, forgotten. On the inside, the children of the forest succumbed to the lure of the mafia, swelling the ranks of the Blood Brothers in order to feel alive and in touch with the outside world.

Luciano and I were like lepers, *tingiuti*, untouchables. Walking corpses. If no one approached us, it meant we'd been marked as people to avoid.

We understood.

Our enemies were powerful, numerous. We were down, dead, buried.

The Blood Brothers had already held us a funeral with empty coffins.

But the isolation helped us, fortifying our resistance. We wouldn't give up until we were staring down the wrong side of a shotgun. Our ancestors, indomitable hunters, had withstood the Greeks and the Romans. We only had to face one ordinary don.

We would wake up early, eat, exercise, shower, and go

down for air. Hot or cold out, the weather didn't matter. Then we went back upstairs to cook something. Then back outside again, and back in, then some reading, dinner, the evening news, and bedtime.

Every day was the same; a year passed in a flash. My brother came only rarely, while my five sisters would take the train from Rome for Thursday visiting hours. My sisters would take turns visiting, but my mother's presence was a constant. Luciano had no relatives, so we asked and were granted permission for him to accompany me to see mine.

Every Thursday morning, right on time, we waited, cleanly shaven, by the bulletproof glass for the agent to summon us.

We hadn't spent so much time with our family in years. We hid our pain and carried on. Our sisters spoke to us about their work and, with ever-lessening embarrassment, about their love lives; they were entitled to their happiness, and it made us happy. They hadn't chosen to be related to me, but as family they gave us all their affection, far more than we deserved.

The preliminary hearing came less than a year after our arrest. Everything unfolded in a single day: we declared ourselves innocent and requested an expedited trial. The prosecutor denied it and scheduled our first trial hearing before a panel of judges for six months later. They cuffed us again and reattached the leash, then yanked us out of the defendants' cage and out of the courtroom. They could have taken their time; we had no one waiting in the corridor for them to fend off, I thought.

I was wrong. I saw that light gray raincoat, cinched at the waist with a belt. Even the officer was surprised. The woman, who softly asked if she could speak to me, was not the kind of person who would have approached a delinquent like me. The officer was dumbfounded, and Giulia took the opportunity to hug me.

"You've lost weight," she said.

"You, too," I replied.

"I sent you a letter," she added. "Read it."

The officer coughed, feigning embarrassment. "We have to go, miss." He jerked me hard; the leash tensed and I trotted behind him like a dog.

People's eyes came to rest on our wrists as we were marched through the labyrinth of the courthouse, and we read in their souls their hate, pity, commiseration, indifference, joy. At first we felt humiliated, but after the first few times we stopped caring.

A van waited in the courtyard to bring us back to our cell. The return was awful—as awful as our arrival had been. They kept us handcuffed and locked us in separate cages inside the armored Ducato. We couldn't see outside. We arrived feeling dizziness and nausea that didn't wear off until the evening. The officer who escorted us back to our block watched smugly as we staggered along.

Among the various police units, the detention officers may have been the least depraved. They were certainly the most frustrated, and they suffered more than the others. Like us, they were always in prison; they endured and dished out insults, and they were ostracized and had no one but themselves to spend time with, even on the outside. It was a hard job. There were often more suicides among the officers than the prisoners; we would eventually get out, while they were serving a life sentence. They locked us up because they had to, not out of choice.

They were officers of the law, but when they explained what they did, people would call them "jailers" before they could finish. It made them fume; they considered it an insult. We prisoners pejoratively referred to them as guards, and they secretly called us *camosci*, antelope, since we were beasts to be herded.

Beatings were rare, as was any physical violence; the worst part was the boredom, the silence, and the jangling of keys. The lights were on day and night; there were eyes on you no matter what you did. The taps ran for a few seconds at a time before you had to press the button again. Touching the popcorn walls drew blood. Searches were conducted daily. Worst of all, you were confined to a ten-by-seven-foot cell for twenty hours each day.

But man has an almost infinite capacity to adapt; without

it, we would have been hanging from the bars in less than a week.

A few days after our hearing, the letter arrived. Actually, there were two letters for me, and the usual five for Luciano. I waited impatiently as the agent opened them, removed their contents, and scanned the pages. I knew which one was Giulia's before I saw the name of the sender; the paper smelled of her. At breakfast, she had a habit of slathering toast with wild honey, and it always ended up on her hands. She had written to me in the morning, before washing up. I liked to see her in the morning; she was more beautiful then, before she put on her makeup. After breakfast, she would come give me a kiss before locking herself in the bathroom. Her honeyed lips would adhere to mine, and when she pulled away, she left the sweet scent just under my nose.

I gave Luciano the letters from my five sisters, who wrote more to him than to me, along with the other letter, also addressed to me, which had a strange stamp and whose sender's name sounded fake. I locked myself in the bathroom to better feel Giulia's presence and only emerged a long while later, content as I hadn't been for some time.

Luciano handed me the letter. It was from Yussuf, the boy who had been wounded on our mission in Germany. He had heard the news and was suffering with us.

I could picture him in front of me, on the pier of Porto

Empedocle, departing for Lebanon with that scarlet rose on his face.

Someone on the outside still thought of us. "Maybe we didn't only sow hatred," I said aloud.

Luciano looked at me. "Maybe," he said, and went back to reading my sisters' secrets.

Outside it started to pour; the sky had darkened. The officer on duty, who was from Salerno, strode past our cell doors, slamming his keys against the bars. "Air!" he shouted, convinced no one would go down to the courtyard in that weather. At our cell, number seventeen, his keys escaped his grasp. When they hit the floor, the roar on the block overcame the sound of the rain. Everyone approached their bars to find out who the lucky cell was.

"Seventeen!" the fucker roared.

There was a belief among the convicts that dropped keys were a sign of freedom, and they hoped for it to happen every time an officer passed their cells. For the fall to count, it had to be an accident.

The detention officer, Catiello Cecere, picked up the keys, saw we were ready to go outside, opened our cell, and smiled. "I did it on purpose. This is your freedom," he said in Salentino, making himself heard throughout the block.

We arrived alone in the courtyard, took off our wool hats, and began to walk back and forth in our fresh air under the deluge. We were visible from the windows of our section and those of the two upper floors.

Dozens of eyes were on us, including those of the other children of the forest in chains. Some of the inmates hated us, others secretly cheered us on and often slipped us notes with greetings and encouragement. When the prison guard was a friend, they would secretly slip us food from our land.

We paced in the rain. A demon still burned inside of us. We would make it swallow its hatred.

BLACK
SOULS

Of the tales that poor Bino used to tell us on those winter evenings, his face transfigured by the flames of the fire, the one about Kyria was perhaps the most far-fetched. And often, at night, it filled my dreams with pagan altars that still dripped with the blood of the beasts offered to the gods, the smoking ashes and the great sacrificial fires that had once burned throughout the night.

Kyria was the people's *Meddix* and the greatest Oscan warrior that had ever lived. He was just over forty years old, and had managed to keep his people alive for more than twenty years. Now he was tired. Their ranks had been decimated by disease and famine—and, above all, by the wickedness of men. They had fought and won their wars against the Etruscans, the Opici, the Aurunci, the Samnites, and the Romans. Kyria had a dream, which was to see his people at peace, herding animals and hunting boar.

He invoked the gods: "Fathers, put an end to this

massacre." Then, a sign: the roar of hooves echoed throughout the valley. A herd of small wild cows appeared. They marched past the huts as they crossed the village. The herd was headed south.

Kyria instantly knew they were marching in the direction of a new life.

The Oscans followed the cows into springtime, crossing mountains whose woods grew intricate and impenetrable. Beeches, firs, pines, all impeded their view of the landscape; all they could see was the ground, which was still covered by a dazzling white carpet of snow.

On their descent they came to a halt. The landscape unfolded into a vast plain with a mighty river that branched off into countless gentle streams. The Oscans finally saw springtime; Kyria had achieved his dream of leading his people to a fertile valley.

Now they could admire the majesty of the mountain they'd descended: it gave origin to the river and life, and they called it the Atioca. Kyria ordered the village to be built on a hillside overlooking the valley.

Long years of peace descended upon the fierce warriors and softened their habits and their lives. The gods had chosen them. Kyria grew convinced that he would not die in battle and abandoned his sword.

Then there arrived a band of Greek scouts, who found an unarmed people. That night the Greeks returned in full force, attacking the unarmed Oscans, who by then were shadows of the warriors they'd once been. Kyria awoke with a searing pain in his chest and, to the astonishment of the soldier who had pierced his heart with a dagger, he leapt up and ran outside, where he witnessed his entire dream in flames.

Only then did he realize that the blade had killed him before he'd even gotten out of bed. He collapsed at the feet of his assassin.

A few Oscans managed to flee the massacre and take refuge by the Atioca. Meanwhile, the Greeks began to enjoy Kyria's paradise, however fleetingly.

The earth trembled from the wrath of the gods. Long minutes of convulsions followed one after the other. They lasted throughout the night until dawn. The sun opened its eyes on a different world. The valley had almost completely disappeared. It was sunken, veined with immense faults. The mountainsides overlooking the valley had crumbled. The only thing still intact, and even more impressive than before, was the Atioca. The river, which until that day had flowed sweetly into streams, had condensed into a single, impetuous torrent, pouring into one of the deepest canyons that had opened on the plain before winding back on itself in a semicircle. The few Greeks who survived the earthquake were massacred by the surviving Oscans, who had immediately recalled their warrior past. And what remained of Kyria's victorious people went to settle on the Atioca. They resumed hunting and grazing flocks, renouncing all their comforts, determined to isolate themselves from the world forever.

The valley, which had once been kind, had transformed into a cluster of hostile and impenetrable mountains.

For years, no one dared to cross the river that the gods had created to protect the Oscans. That river was called Apo-Osci-Potamos and for the children of the forest, its waters represented the line between good and evil.

I could hear Bino telling me the story again in my dream before I was awoken by the evening news.

It was 8 P.M.; I always watched thirty minutes of the evening news before going to bed. For a year and a half, each day had insisted on being the same as the one before it.

We listened to their lead story, Luciano stretched out on the lower bunk and I perched on the metal slab bolted to the wall, which served as a table. Most of the airtime was dedicated to one of the recurring pan-Arabian peace conferences. Rome had offered to host the most recent one; delegates had come from all the Arab countries to draft a peace plan for the tormented lands of Palestine.

The broadcast ended with an exclusive interview with the head delegate from one of the participating countries. The overly excited journalist posed obvious questions, prompting a saccharine monologue by the delegate, a man dressed in black and white who spoke good Italian. Taking a pious tone, he implored his Palestinian brothers to lay down their arms and engage in a dialogue with their life-long enemy so that they could enjoy a peaceful future together.

His face was smooth, perfectly shaven, and his appearance

was neat and affable. But these elements hardly managed to conceal the soldier lurking behind his businesslike facade. His words extolled goodness, but he emanated evil and death. His eyes were hypnotic, demanding attention. I was struck with a feeling I couldn't name.

I went to bed hoping to find my way back to Bino's tales, but instead I entered a nightmare. I saw Kyria on the ground with the gash in his chest; the soldier who had killed him smiled wickedly and his face took on the features of the Arab delegate. And then I finally recognized him: he was the bearded leader of the Arabs I'd met in the Sierra Nevada.

The vision jolted me awake.

For the children of the forest, evil always came from the east. The last time Sasà and I had met that Arab, it was to inform him that we would be closing our trafficking operation to work on another project. That time, we'd met him in a town in France that had been founded a few millennia earlier by the Romans. He embraced us and bid us goodbye, with the promise that he would pray to God for us and our dream. But his eyes had not been as kind as his words.

And in fact, what had happened to us couldn't have been entirely the work of Don Peppino Zacco's *picciotti* thugs, who were more adept at weaponry than details. The hits on Santoro and Natalia had been executed by perfectionists, artists of death. Zacco dealt in buckshot, not barbiturates and car accidents.

I pushed the thoughts out of my mind, closed my eyes, and tried to get back to Bino's stories.

"Kyria, Kyria . . ." Sweet Atéa shook the corpse of the Meddix. Her tears rained down on Kyria's face and pooled in his open eyes before descending the sides of his nose in rivulets, mixing with the blood on his chest.

"Kyria."

I started awake. It was Luciano. Only he called me Kyria. I'd been named according to tradition; the first-born male in a goatherd family was always named after his paternal grandfather. So I, like my grandfather, had been named Kyria after the father of the Oscans.

"Get up. They're coming for us," he said. It was the morning of our first hearing. After a year and a half, we would finally meet the judges on the panel that would decide our fate.

If accused of the offense in article 416b of the Criminal Code, or in articles 74, 73, and 80 of Presidential Decree 309/90, all violations related to drugs and organized crime, you could wait up to ten years before receiving a final sentence. Although constitutionally innocent, you remained in pre-trial detention, because alternative measures to prison weren't provided for under the law. You ended up in separate, high-security blocks, which meant twenty hours locked in a cell, no cultural or sporting activities, and no penitentiary benefits. At dawn, you were awakened by the infernal noise of an iron rod slamming against each bar of your cell. You went out for air, you were searched, you returned to your cell, you were searched again. Family visiting hours, search, lawyer interview, search. Trial, search. A few officers appeared in your cell: search, pants to the floor, flex. You came back to your cell from the fresh air to find all of your things on the floor. You spent the day tidying up, you went to take a shower, then returned to find everything on the floor again.

Only the severely twisted could hope to survive.

On the outside, everyone assumed that anyone who was doing time must have done something wrong. On the inside, we always said that only the innocent ended up in jail. Both were true. The cops made their arrests in certain environments where purer souls ran scarce. They picked up the kind of people who had committed every possible crime, but often not the one they'd been accused of.

The guilty didn't complain about the treatment they received; the innocent were tormented by having to pay for something they hadn't done, especially when they had done so many other things.

When someone first ends up in prison, they don't feel like a prisoner; they're still waiting for a miracle. After five or six years, the brain begins its decline and they lose interest in everything. Only poison remains.

We were caged like animals at the zoo—though they had

done nothing wrong apart from being wild animals. The hardship was greatest for prisoners from the South, especially if you were Calabrian, and worst of all if you were from Locride. No justification could influence the stubborn morals of the judges, prosecutors, and policemen. We were the scum of humanity, immoral and amoral beasts, and we existed only to be taken down. Guys who returned from their trials with sentences of less than twenty years would celebrate. With early parole they could be out in fifteen and, naturally, go back to committing more crimes.

The prisoners belonged to one of two categories: the consciously bad and the unconsciously bad. The latter could be rehabilitated; they'd done wrong as a result of emulation, marginalization, misery, or by force. They weren't aware of the evil they were doing or its consequences. Four or five years on the inside would have sufficed to make them as docile as lambs. Burying them under decades of prison time, however, made monsters of them. The consciously bad always understood the gravity of what they were doing and its consequences. They didn't accept rules and limits; they simulated docility but in reality they were true monsters, and they wouldn't stop until someone killed them.

Thus, wolves and lambs were held together in the same pen under the pretense of improving society.

When the agents arrived, we were waiting at the bars. They made us undress. After the search, we went down to the holding cells. The escort arrived; he searched us; we got into the armored car. We were left in our transit cages in the basement of the courthouse. We were searched again and led to the defendants' cage in the courtroom.

They took off our handcuffs and leashes and we looked our judges in the eyes.

Two other cases were heard before ours began. Luciano waved to our two young defenders, who had been assigned to us after we'd been renounced by our supposedly indisposed luminary. They arrived in front of the cage. They seemed sharp enough, or so Luciano said after a long conversation with them, little of which I grasped. They took their seats with an air of satisfaction, and after a few hours had passed, our case was called.

One of our boys took the floor. There was, he said, an absolutely pre-eminent preliminary matter that had to be addressed with regard to the case. A very recent ruling by the Constitutional Court had recognized the conflict of interest of anyone who had in any way evaluated the initial detention order in a judicial capacity. Whoever had issued the defendant's warrant for arrest or rejected their request for bail, assuming the accusations were meaningful, could not serve as a judge in the defendant's trial, having already demonstrated their bias regarding their guilt.

The presiding judge deemed the question worthy of exploring, and postponed the hearing, having no immediate access to the text of the Court's ruling, nor the proof that any panel members had expressed prognostic judgments of guilt.

Our lawyer, red in the face, requested the floor. He noted that one of the defendants was in possession of the text in question.

Luciano was authorized to hand over a folder he had brought with him to the clerk, who came to the front of the cage to collect it. He'd had the prison prepare copies for the prosecution, the defense, and the judges.

Everyone read attentively. The prosecutor opposed the acceptance of the text, given its unofficial origins. Our lawyers insisted that the evidence be admitted. The panel withdrew and came back with a Solomonic—and intelligent—decision: the documents weren't admitted, and the prosecutor's request was accepted. But one of the three judges on the panel noted his conflict of interest and recused himself from the case.

The trial was postponed pending the foregone acceptance of the judge's recusal by the Court of Appeal and for his substitution to be arranged.

One month later we found ourselves standing before a new panel of judges, and in the place of the previous judge we found a heart-stopping blonde. Her face betrayed her suffering; the dark circles under her eyes told of her sleepless nights. It was Chiara, poor Santoro's wife.

Another case was called first, then ours. The young lawyers approached Luciano and everyone watched the scene unfold, concealing their curiosity.

Luciano began the consultation. I, who had no role in the

matter, dedicated myself to the only thing that interested me: Giulia, who sat among the public.

I embraced her gaze and we conducted a silent dialogue that would continue until the end of the hearing. I heard the judges and lawyers in the distance. The court opened the proceedings for our case, the useless procedural skirmishes instigated by our defense team to demonstrate their mastery of the doctrine were soon overturned, and the hearing began. The prosecutor requested a reading of the indictments and the admission of evidence. The defense noted a few witnesses and made their more serious requests.

They stated that the defendants had always maintained their innocence, claiming that someone had hidden the drugs in their car to frame them. It emerged that the accusations were exclusively found in the declarations made by the arresting officers. It would be useful to engage a court expert who could detect fingerprints to establish who the drugs belonged to, they said. It would also be useful to acquire telephone records of calls made to headquarters in the hours before the arrest.

The prosecutor became cyanotic; his reply was venomous. The defense was questioning the honesty of our faithful public servants.

The back-and-forth that followed was exhaustive, Luciano making continuous suggestions while Giulia and I traveled off together to other worlds.

The panel entered the council chamber to deliberate.

A few hours passed before the bell announced their return. The battle lines were drawn on the faces of the judges who sat on either side of the presiding judge.

The requests of the defense are accepted, Chiara ceded.

A handful of simple referral hearings were held, and after a few months the trial heated up. Our fingerprints hadn't been found on any of the packages, and in fact the last people to handle them had used gloves. Phone records of incoming calls revealed one in particular that warned the police about a large cocaine stash in a car. The license plate, color, and type of car were indicated, along with the street where it was parked. The voice had a strong Arabic inflection.

The grinning policemen who had arrested us sat down one at a time before the court. In their testimonies they'd claimed that the operation had been the result of laborious investigations that had taken months, aimed at monitoring our movements from opposite our apartment on via Spartaco and trailing our car.

Our lawyers demonstrated, through witnesses and documents, that the house and the car had been in use by us, the defendants, for less than a week. The witnesses for the prosecution left the courtroom in a daze.

After a few more months, we lodged our final requests: full acquittal, our representatives demanded. Despite the evidence that had emerged, the public prosecutor insisted on our conviction. But his request was meeker, and he suggested that the standard twenty-four year sentence be reduced by one third, in the interest of a shorter trial, which had been requested but not granted at the preliminary hearing. A total of sixteen years in jail. It was nothing.

Giulia looked at me in despair, burst into tears, and ran out of the courtroom. There was a buzz from the audience, to which some of our escorting officers also contributed. The presiding judge silenced everyone. The panel withdrew to deliberate.

The judges' faces announced the ruling before they did. The presiding judge was impenetrable, as usual. The judge to his left was livid, and Chiara was radiant: article 530, paragraph two, acquittal. Under the old ordinance, this meant insufficient evidence, the only concession the judges had made to the prosecution.

We returned to our cell on our leashes for the last time. We placed the belongings that had accompanied us for those two years in black trash bags; according to prison superstition, we got rid of anything that could bring bad luck.

We said goodbye to the few boys who had been our friends and went out into the evening.

A light autumn rain greeted us, as did Gino, Giulio, Tonino, Ciccio, and Giulia. A little world of people who loved us.

We ate in a *trattoria* for truck drivers outside Milan. Our heads were spinning; we couldn't stand all the noises.

People on the inside don't think they've left the real world, they think they know how things and people are on the outside. But once you're out you realize that everything moves so fast, at twice the speed. You have to catch up slowly, and for a few months you sleep on a cot like the one where you spent so many nights. You wake up thinking you can hear the sound of bars.

The others stayed with some of Tonino's friends who were still in the area. I went to Giulia's.

We didn't speak. We were one, she followed my lead and didn't ask questions.

After a few days, we cautiously sought out Anna and Chiara. They showered us with a thousand warm greetings and bits of advice before they'd even let us through their front door; they, too, were a part of our world.

We hung around Milan for a while. The joy, the desire to feel alive that had filled the city before—it had all vanished. Now, the Milanese lived as shut-ins. The outside world made them more and more afraid. The paladins once they'd praised had delivered a heap of trash instead of the new future they'd promised.

We left it behind us, that past that could no longer return. We drove south to the mountain kingdom of Stefano Bennaco and his family. We were safe there.

We resumed contact with our land and our people; our minds began to function normally again, by our standards.

———

In the mountain village of our countryside, there were about ten houses, but only four or five families, all related. It was where the last goatherds lived, survivors of the progress the outsiders had tried to force on us.

Back in the village, Luciano avoided drinking, because when he drank he grew spiteful, and until the fumes of alcohol evaporated along with the demon that possessed him, he would repeat the same speech endlessly, to anyone and everyone.

"When we lived among ourselves we were a quiet people, everyone played a role, we respected shared rules, we helped one another. Each of us had his own territory, of which he was the absolute master; he decided where to graze, where to set up the fold, where to grow crops, where to cut trees, where to raze the land, he did whatever he pleased. Anyone who invaded someone else's territory knew what he was up against and accepted the consequences. He would pay for his mistakes; first and foremost, his own family would hold him accountable. Once upon a time, we had very few and certain rules, printed from our genetic code. The masters of our world, the pagan gods and the Holy Father, had handed them down to us, telling Kyria how to lead the way. We wanted to live in peace, to watch over our herds. The Greeks arrived to destroy our paradise and from then on we decided to live in hell to repel other greedy conquerors. Only God's army had come in peace, in the form of the solitary and pious Basilian monks. The Bourbons came looking for us in order to impose their tariffs and rules, and they created an army of Blood Brothers to subdue us from the inside. The Savoy followed them, allowing the gangsters to carry on and introducing new tariffs and new rules. The Black Shirts arrived to annex us for the Empire to which Italy was entitled, and we got a taste of their batons and castor oil. The Republic sent us out into the world to break our backs for a piece of bread. They needed manpower to fuel their progress and depopulated our mountains, by force or by enticing us with money and the mirage of a better life. Only in our forests could we be normal people; out of our habitat, we were like beasts in captivity, wild animals foaming at the mouth. What did they expect to do, tame us? They came looking for us, not the other way around. We were happy with our black bread, our hunger, our diseases, our backward ways; we didn't want their help. They came to our pastures to hang up signs prohibiting hunting, prohibiting fishing, prohibiting grazing, prohibiting everything that made us free. Why couldn't a thousand-year-old people be allowed to choose their own way of life on their own land? We didn't want their integration, their progress, their language, their money. They opened the door to the devil."

Luciano could have burnt the world down in those moments. "What did I say?" he would always ask the next morning. "Nothing. They were the ones who started it," I would answer. Then he would laugh and become his usual self again.

———

We were back in our mountains, free again. We weren't kids anymore. We'd been plotting thefts and murders for years. We wouldn't stop until we hit a wall.

Now it was the Blood Brothers' turn. Traitors to their own people, sell-outs to the established order. In the mountains, we could speak freely about our plans, unlike in jail, with the cameras and bugs everywhere.

I shared my observations with Luciano, and we agreed.

Yussuf had continued to send letters this whole time, letters which always ended with a maxim or a verse from the Koran or the Bible. Those closing phrases contained a hidden message. Luciano was able to decipher them easily. The most important ones read: *The best father goes crazy if possessed by the demon of power, he comes to kill children who do not support him*, and *Cain followed Satan and left his brother to die.*

The father was the head of their faction, the source of the evil. He had mowed down everyone who stood in the way of our annihilation.

With our decision to stop trafficking after one last trip, we had signed our own death warrants. Everything had to proceed at all costs, and Luciano and I had become obstacles to the cash flow he'd been enjoying for years, the fruits of our labor. The Arabs he'd sent to kill us hadn't had the guts to take us out, remembering the risks we'd taken to save Yussuf.

Instead, they'd planted drugs in our car and called the police as a way of sparing us. They paid for it with their lives.

We had a clear picture of the situation in our heads. Tonino's men informed us that the same stuff we used to distribute around Milan was still in circulation. The Arab leader, after eliminating Alfio, Santoro, and Natalia, had reeled in Sasà and Luigi after they'd escaped arrest, and he'd somehow convinced them to keep working. Down south, Zacco took advantage of the opportunity and delivered his blow. If he'd succeeded in full, the plan would have wiped us out forever.

That was our theory.

It was all confirmed by what we knew about Zacco: Don Peppino hadn't let up; one of Tonino's boys who had infiltrated his ranks said he'd lost his mind with rage at our sentencing. "Those bastards, out after two years. What kind of fucking justice is this? With all those drugs they should have gotten thirty, and now they're free to cook up more tragedies. We have to make the first move."

Zacco wanted to hit us first, but we didn't let him.

We each wore an earpiece connected to a transceiver. We were sitting in two separate cars, tucked away on a path hidden by a high cane thicket a hundred yards from the highway. Tonino was driving one car, with Luciano at his side, while I sat in the back.

Giulio drove the car ahead of us, carrying Ciccio and Gino. I imagined them joking around and listening to all the hits on the radio. The three boys were carefree in the face of death.

Our friend gave us the go: "Blue follows red." There were two cars, and Zacco was in the blue one.

We reached the intersection and let them pass.

They were speeding, on their way to a meeting with other bosses from neighboring villages.

The boys passed them, flanked the red car and opened fire. At the same time, Luciano let loose on the occupants in the front seats of the blue car. I was about to do the same to Don Peppino, but I stopped myself. We got out of our cars and shot each bodyguard in the head.

Don Peppino got out quietly, turned his back to us, and said, "Make it fast, you little shits."

We shot him with gusto, reloading and unloading so many times we would have had to scoop up his body with a shovel. When Giulio and Ciccio arrived, they joined in the massacre. I went to stop them and Luciano blocked me. "Leave it," I read on his lips.

Stefano, stationed a few miles ahead of us, warned us that the patrols were on their way. We calmly climbed back into our cars and slipped onto the mountain road.

"Why?" I asked Luciano, as we were driving. He turned to look at me. I didn't need to finish my question. He knew I was referring to the boys; he had wanted them to shoot at Zacco, too.

"Do you remember Don Vincenzo's memoirs?"

"Uh-huh."

"Do you remember how many strips of paper I kept?"

"Uh-huh."

"This is the third," he said, handing it to me.

Don Peppino Zacco reported to me on the death of engineer Bonasira, I read.

I rolled up the strip and put it in my mouth. Giulio and Ciccio Bonasira didn't need to know about their father; they could continue to rail against him for having abandoned them to go mess around who knows where. I thought about keeping it from Minna, too, so she could still enjoy the sympathy she received for having been abandoned.

Luciano and I had been working on that act of revenge for years, and perhaps for our whole lives. It had just been the two of us, we hadn't told a soul, not even Sasà or Luigi. In chasing after the money, Zacco had gotten a head start on us, but now we'd overtaken him. We'd spent years training a group of boys, helping them, giving them loads of money. Recently, we'd brought Tonino into the plan, and he'd managed the boys after our arrest. At our behest, many of them had joined the Blood Brothers, even though they each had an account to settle with them. They showed their gratitude up to the end, informing us of everything they saw or heard.

After Zacco's death we only touched the most dangerous leaders and assassins. They were our enemies; they'd brought death to our doors.

Don Santino Cozza was one of Zacco's most loyal allies; he had a healthy cohort made up of very close relatives. After the death of his friend, he'd barricaded himself in his home to plot his bloody response, surrounding himself with impenetrable security measures. He lived in a kind of fort with high walls, cameras, and ferocious dogs to guard the grounds. Access was limited to his brother's sons, who served as his guards, and to his young wife. Occasionally he received one of his young soldiers, who would be permitted to enter alone after a careful search made by Cozza's nephews. He lived on the ground floor, and the windows were barred.

After a month of useless stakeouts, we postponed our ambush, waiting for the defensive mesh to loosen.

Giulio, Ciccio, and Gino, however, had gotten a little carried away; they knew our objectives and often acted in anticipation of our orders. They belonged to a more reckless generation than ours when it came to death and managed to outdo us, which was no easy feat.

They studied Don Santino and identified his weaknesses. Cozza was about fifty years old, and had become a widower a few years before, when leukemia had taken away the mother of his two daughters. The latter, already married, didn't live with him. To remedy his loneliness he allowed himself to stretch the honored society's rules, bringing a young Romanian woman home to keep him company. Lorenza was from Craiova, a large city in Romania. She had landed in Turin searching for good luck, and ended up in a nightclub run by one of Cozza's men. Before the customers could enjoy her, Don Santino offered her wads of cash and brought her home with him to occupy his empty bridal chamber.

Beautiful women abounded in the village, but none of them were six-foot-tall redheads with green eyes. Lorenza was a rock in a stagnant pond; the boss fell madly in love with her and naturally became incredibly jealous.

Despite the terror that Cozza inspired, it was difficult for any man to resist the temptation of glancing at that supernatural creature. Several went further, venturing a compliment to the diva; and in this way, from time to time, some daring young man would disappear without a trace.

But for all the Don's power and imposing personality, he was defenseless against his statuesque Romanian, who often left the compound at the godfather's behest. Don Santino required her to go shopping alone every morning, because the boss didn't even trust his own nephews when it came to the meat. She always left in a huge armored jeep, draped in a dark coat that reached her ankles and wearing sunglasses big enough to hide her face, with a headscarf knotted over her dazzling copper hair. Of the shops along the coast, the last, obligatory stop was Pasquale Panazza's bakery. At precisely half past twelve, the baker wrapped up her bread, hot out of the traditional wood oven that he fired with olive branches. The lady wouldn't have it prepared any other way.

Before Lorenza had come along, Pasquale would bake

all night, sell the last of his bread by eight-thirty in the morning and go back to sleep until the afternoon. The Romanian forced him to change his habits. Pasquale brought a large bed to his store and placed it in the toasty little room behind the oven. That way, he could sleep until half past eleven, get up, and prepare the goods to be delivered on time to his one and only midday customer before going back to bed. He did everything mechanically, his eyes half-closed.

When he heard the door open, he reflexively bundled the bread. He couldn't have been less interested in looking at the woman in question; he preferred his own voluptuous Antonia. All he cared about was sleep. That day, when Ciccio prodded his chin with the barrel of the Belgian-made Walter PPK 9mm, Pasquale made a gesture as if to swat away a fly. He had to force himself to focus on the image of the hooded youth, who pushed him into the back room and cuffed him to the foot of his comfortable bed; he almost wanted to thank him for taking him there.

Lorenza made her usual bold entrance, swathed in a cloud of her French perfume, the only one she used. She maintained her regal air even as she followed the young man with the gun.

In the wheat-scented back room, the baker was already snoring away by the warmth of the oven. Lorenza was disappointed when she realized that all the robber wanted was her overcoat, her sunglasses, and her scarf, but she didn't resist.

She flung her overcoat across the room, and before Ciccio could retrieve it, she had undressed completely.

Pasquale was sure he was dreaming. No woman could really be made like that, with such a slender waist, breasts pointing to the sky, silk instead of skin; nor was it normal for men to have a monstrosity like Ciccio's between their legs. Even if it was just a dream, Pasquale wanted to ask his Antonia to try the same position.

After Ciccio had fallen nearly half an hour behind schedule, Giulio and Gino began to worry. Santino was worried, too, and the cell phone in Lorenza's coat pocket began to howl angrily.

Ciccio looked at Lorenza, not sure what to do; she signaled for him to pass her the phone, which she answered in a brooding voice: "I'm coming, baby, the baker was late."

"You're fucking someone else!" replied Don Cozza.

Every day at that hour, a few kids passed by the bakery on their way home for lunch. That day, they looked on appreciatively as the Romanian got in her jeep without deigning to glance in their direction and drove off to the sound of the Fugees' "Killing Me Softly." The boys rushed off to a lunch that was growing cold.

When the jeep reached Don Zacco's, Ciccio passed the point where his companions were waiting in ambush, lowered the window, and gave them the finger. "Fuck you!" his friends shouted at him. He pressed the remote control and opened the bunker's outer gate. The nephews knew that their uncle was spying on them from a window and let their beautiful aunt pass through without looking twice at her.

The second button opened the door to the garage that led into the villa. Then Ciccio crossed an antechamber and entered the living room, where the pathetic lover had his back turned; he'd arranged flowers and lit romantic candles, and now he was setting the table.

"That bastard Pasquale," he said. "Tomorrow I'll have him shot in the legs."

Santino was sulking. He expected the woman's arms to wrap around him from behind, for her soft lips to make him forget about her delay; Santino had a gift in his pocket, as he'd had for every day they'd spent together and would have for every day to come.

His daughters should have been happy; that day, all of his spending of their inheritances was put to an end.

Santino didn't understand the reason for the bite he felt on his back, the teeth that sank into his flesh. The long blade of the Opinel no. 12 slipped easily between the vertebrae of his dorsal column, paralyzing him instantly. But before he died, Ciccio made sure Santino knew that Lorenza had screamed with pleasure in the arms of his killer, and that she was now locked up naked with that bastard Pasquale, who was not, as he had believed, the adulterer.

The nephews saw their aunt leave again and figured their strange relatives were having one of their usual lovers' spats. They were left to unwittingly guard a corpse.

In the early afternoon, Antonia arrived with her one hundred and eighty pounds of sensuality to make coffee for Pasquale, who, upon awaking from his nap, always had a special urge to see her. It took four people to restrain the baker's wife, who was sending her husband and his Romanian whore to the next life with the baker's paddle. It hadn't just been bread that woman had been getting from Pasquale, she screamed. Stories began to spread before the envied Don Juan recovered from his beating and managed to explain what he had been doing in bed naked with Lorenza. People only believed the baker's story after Don Santino's body was found and the farce suddenly turned to tragedy.

There had never been such a sensational execution, and it caught everyone by surprise, including us. The boys became feared beyond measure; they rarely went out, but when they were seen it meant they were on the hunt, and everyone waited to hear the name of the next victim.

Over the years they had created their own network of friends, boys their own age who worshiped them. They became black souls unlike any before them; only Sante, perhaps, could have compared. They had adapted to the time and place better than we had. And they'd pulled off the whole thing by themselves.

There was a kind of revolt in the opposing camp, and the Blood Brothers were in disarray; in just a short time a dozen of their most important representatives had made their journeys to the great beyond. Many who had answered to them began to evade their control, and others found the courage to settle long-pending accounts. And now there were hits from all directions, executed by anyone and everyone. It made for a sort of free zone, without the influence of the mafia; nobody answered to anyone if they weren't answering to us.

After a few years the war died down, assassinations tapered off. To assert our presence, it was enough to make an example of someone only once in a while.

In our territory we were safe. We formed alliances with groups scattered throughout the countryside, out of the mob's range. People began to turn to us with all kinds of problems. We helped everyone without asking for anything in return; they were our people. Petty crime ceased; we had more work than the *carabinieri* and the high commissioner put together. But the evil done by the Blood Brothers couldn't be erased.

In the Aurora, Luciano and I became kids again. I remembered how his big, brown eyes always grew teary during the Christmas holidays. He never wanted to go home; there was no one waiting for him. His mother used to wander out in her perennial black garb to collect him. She always found him sitting next to the small monument that marked the spot where his father, a simple postman, had died.

The Aurora was near our town's *carabinieri* barracks. Growing up, we would often see Don Peppino Zacco making his daily drop-ins; sometimes he would notice us, approach, and drop some coins in Luciano's hand. "Buy yourself some nuts, little orphan," he'd say. He'd look up in the direction of Minna's balcony. "Greetings, Mrs. Bonasira." Then he would go off in his car, which was always driven by some young soldier. Minna refused to go outside; Luciano's mother, who always watched from the window, would go out, take the coins from her son's hand, and throw them away. We understood who was evil before we knew the facts; there were many orphans like Luciano who roamed the villages.

The Aurora was its own microcosm in the tiny world of a village in Locride. Sixteen families, dozens of souls joined by a bond that transcended that of blood. All for one and one for all. United in a common destiny. One big family, sharing all their joys and pain. The kids got up at dawn in the summer and played until they collapsed from exhaustion. A break for lunch and then back to the courtyard until sunset. Dusk in the Aurora was an event both magical and strange. The kids would stop playing; the women dragged out their chairs and waited for the men to come back from the mountains. Even the widows in black sat out by their doors, though they had no one to wait for. The little ones would study them with compassion, without understanding. But they would understand later. This was how the boys of the Aurora grew up, drinking from the fountain of hatred and thirsting for revenge. And this was how the boys of the Aurora learned to transform their pain into satisfaction. They walked the hellish streets and took their darkness elsewhere, to taint other houses and other women. The boys of the Aurora grew up at dusk, when the glare of the sun could no longer hide the harshness of life. And in the end, dawn in the Aurora never arrived; the day became night and the night swallowed everything.

We weren't aware of it at the time, but that's what had set us on our path. What we were, all that we had, and all that we did had been born of those childhood scenes. So much violence over so many years, all because Don Peppino had decided to take out one old peasant who held a job he had reserved for one of his own friends.

Firm in his political ideology and with the law on his side, Luciano's father had obtained his position through a series of whistle-blowing reports, forcing the state to respect his rights and to discount fraudulent claims of others' seniority; as he proudly called it, a poor man's victory. There was no section meeting in which he didn't praise himself for his courage or the example he set. How many lives had that bastard destroyed?

We made it through the war unscathed. But there would be pain just the same, delivered to us by nature herself.

Stefano's son, Cosimo, arrived breathless; his father was

lying on the ground in his goat enclosure, showing no signs of life. We ran with our hearts in our throats and found him with his eyes to the sky, surrounded by his goats. He had just finished the milking and stood to lift the buckets of milk when he collapsed. Now he lay peacefully among the beasts, the milk soaking his clothes; his heart had suddenly given up, without warning.

He died without pain, and we all privately wished for a similar death.

A God-willed death leaves a calm sorrow, easily placated in the arms of a tender wife, or by hugging a small child.

Death delivered by man leaves desert in its wake that all the water in the world can't quench.

Luciano, Tonino, and I buried Stefano, left our contributions to his boys, and parted for Milan. We didn't want to die with pending accounts, and this time the enemy was much more powerful than any other we'd faced.

We stayed with Giannetto, one the boys orphaned by Totò the Blade on Zacco's orders, whom we'd raised in secret. Luciano, who had always kept the books, had been sending gifts and money for years, unbeknownst to even Luigi or Sasà. Giannetto could never betray us. With our blessing and the money we left him, he had continued to traffic cocaine even after our arrest.

He moved large quantities and knew the biggest traffickers. The most important supplier working in Milan was a Calabrian, but unlike us, he was a city boy. He distributed those packages we knew so well, he was our man, so we had Giannetto put in an order for us.

Even though Giannetto could sell a lot, our request for a ton of coke caught him off guard. It took a few months of to-ing and fro-ing. Giannetto made his city boy dealer lie down in the back seat of his car, covered him with a blanket, and took him to an apartment. He placed a series of suitcases on the table, opened them, and told him to count the cash. He would pay in a lump sum on delivery, he said.

The Calabrian took his time. After a few weeks, he scheduled a meeting with Giannetto; he would have to talk it over in person with his bosses, he confessed.

We left for Spain by car, arriving in Denia, a resort town south of Valencia. The meeting was in a typical Valencian restaurant. Giannetto slipped inside and sat down at a table. We positioned ourselves in a cafe across the street.

The traffickers arrived, dead sure of themselves, without scoping the place out much. They were well-dressed, well-groomed; they looked like kids. They introduced themselves to Giannetto and got straight to business; they were so absorbed they didn't even notice us when we passed their table.

We sat at the back of the room, where a waiter quickly jotted down our orders: a double order of *calamares a la plancha* and two San Miguels.

Giannetto suddenly stood up, interrupting the conversation, and gestured in the direction of our table.

The traffickers' boldness disappeared. They aged suddenly in the face of their consciences. They approached us. Luigi cracked a smile, opened his arms for an embrace, which Sasà blocked. He wanted to explain first. Sasà told us everything we wanted to know in a matter of minutes. Then they got up and left with their heads hanging. I felt sorry for them. They'd grown used to the rhythms of their new life; they would forget about us soon enough.

My life and Luciano's had separated from those of Luigi and Sasà, perhaps forever. A piece of us left with them. We had loved them and still did; we did not feel as if we were better than they were. They were certainly doing things right, better than we were; they lived full lives, they enjoyed themselves, this was what they'd wanted. Our path, on the other hand, was marked by a death mission that would have been stupid, as well as impossible, to escape. Our principles, our revenge, our rules, the accounts we had to close—it might all have been bullshit, but our demons carried us to the end.

We silently wished them well; at least they would be spared, and for that we were happy. They would always be our brothers.

We finished our calamari and beer and left. We didn't have the strength to speak. We got into the car and Giannetto took us back to Milan. He took care of everything we needed for the trip.

The coded letters Yussuf had written us contained a phone number; we contacted him and, after a few days, met him as he strolled out of the Malpensa airport in Milan. He looked the same as when we'd waved him goodbye from the docks. The scarlet rose on his cheekbone attested to his past as a fighter.

Of the Sierra Nevada boys, he told us, he was one of the few survivors.

Giannetto had gotten us a car, documents, and weapons, which we hid in a car door.

Tonino drove for a while. Then, after we entered France unchecked through Ventimiglia, Luciano took the wheel. We drove along the coast to Marseilles, where we took the A7 into the heart of France. A beautiful Mediterranean landscape accompanied us for a long stretch. Every now and then, we crossed the Rhône, a mass of water that would have been unthinkable for our lands, as it rushed off to embrace the Mediterranean. We passed Avignon and got off the highway at a small town with a Roman name, Arausio, an ancient colony of the empire. We followed the signs for Mount Ventoux. Sasà's information had been detailed, precise.

The stunning villa wasn't hard to find.

It had grown dark. We turned off on a dirt road and slept in the car until our appointment. Our man lived in Paris, where he carried out his political activity, coddled and acclaimed by Westerners, who were perhaps unaware that they'd opened their homes to a butcher. He spent weekends at his country villa at the foot of Mount Ventoux, and would drive back to Paris every Monday at dawn.

At five o'clock in the morning, the great gate opened wide, making way for a luxurious sedan. The lord of death had been gentrified; he felt untouchable in that land, and hadn't bothered with an armored car, escort or weapons, only a chauffeur to attest to his status as a very rich businessman, as well as a champion of peace.

Luciano cut off the road in front of the sedan, which stopped without suspicion. The driver rushed out as if to deliver some government file. Tonino pulled him through the car window with one hand and sent him into the world of dreams with a single shot to the head.

The lord of death looked on, annoyed, as the car door opened. When he realized it was Yussuf and me, a fake smile broke out across his face. "My children," he said, "there are things more valuable than our miserable lives." It was useless. We made him get out and kneel.

In horror, he stared at the shotguns, with their sawed-off muzzles and butts. They stared back at him with their empty eyes, from which one shot after the next began to pour. After two reloads, we lost count. We took the Fiocchi's ammunition from the cartridge cases at our waists. The shotguns roared and spat out lead. With each shot the shortened weapons tried to wriggle out of our grasp and point themselves upwards. Grimly we held the butts in place and kept the muzzles low, directing them at the mangled body. I could taste the gunpowder in my mouth; my eyes were burning.

"Enough!" Tonino shouted.

Never had a death been so liberating. What we left on the asphalt looked more like the remains of an animal dragged under the wheels of a truck than the body of a man.

The demon that had destroyed thousands of lives was now in Muslim hell, if there was one.

We took our time and changed course on the way back; instead of descending France into Italy, we went east. Before noon we had arrived in Nancy, a beautiful bonbon of a town in Lorraine. We parked behind Place Stanislas, a huge square enclosed by high gates and paved with spotless porphyry. It was like going back in time; in the middle stood the statue of Duke Stanislas, who had given the square its name. We sat at the tables of a restaurant that allowed us to observe the town in all her beauty. We ate the *noix St. Jacques*, and after lunch we left the car and headed for the *gare* on foot. The train crossed the entire Moselle and left us in Luxembourg City. We changed trains, taking a series of locals to Germany—Trier, Koblenz, Mannheim, Munich. At nine in the evening we caught a *Euronotte* to Italy through Brenner. At 4:20 A.M. we found ourselves having breakfast in Piazza Medaglie d'Oro, in front of the station in Bologna. In via San Vitale we met a friend of ours and in the evening, after taking Yussuf to the airport, we left for our homeland.

That trip gave us a chance to catch our breath; we'd been going faster than usual, and we weren't kids anymore. But for once in our lives we were also satisfied, fully and without remorse.

It was still dark when we got back; I found Giulia in a deep sleep, enveloped in her perfume. I rested my hand on her belly and jerked it away, terrified; the life inside of her had moved. A small smile escaped her lips; she was due very soon.

For me, it had been nine months of terror. It was said that when the universe wanted to punish a bad man, it struck down what he loved, knowing it was useless to punish his person. The bad man feared nothing for himself, though he was aware of the damage he caused. What he feared most was that his unearthly rage would be directed back at his own children.

Every evening before going to sleep, I would pray to the god of the Christians, the pagan gods of the woods, and above all, to the pious Basilian monk who had transformed pitch into bread for my ancestors, to reserve all evil for me and to spare my wife, my children, Luciano, Gino, Giulio, Ciccio, Tonino and all those dear to me. If comeuppance was due, the originator of the sin should pay, not his accomplices.

I refused to know the sex of the unborn child or hear anything about its health. I made Luciano take Giulia to all of her doctors' appointments. She was the most beautiful creature that had entered our lives, as a wife, mother, sister, friend; she was always smiling, she cooked, cleaned, gave lessons with never a complaint, never a reproach, never a regret. She was aware of the choice she'd made and would have stood by it forever. She became the most important person in each of our lives; no one dared to contradict her, and our love for her was without limits.

And then the day came. We paced up and down the hospital corridors, tense like never before. I wasn't strong enough to enter the delivery room. I went limp. When the midwife called for us, Luciano went in first.

They spent endless minutes inside before the door swung open and Luciano came out holding two bundles tight to his chest: "Everything's fine, including these two little peas."

Twin boys, identical and the spitting image of Giulia; nature still loved us, in spite of everything. I felt a calm like never before; no matter what happened, Giulia wouldn't be alone. I thanked God, the pagan gods, and the Saint. We named them after my father and poor Bino and took them home.

If they'd left us alone, we would have finally buried the hatchet.

But they didn't want to.

The state wanted to avenge the Blood Brothers, who'd been hung out to dry. Secular deception had been eliminated, the Law could no longer get information from our inner circles, and the state was very interested in what was incubating in the hearts of the people of the forest. The centuries-old hierarchy had to be restored.

The official rule of law in those lands had two faces: the serious and sad Captain Randone, and the arrogant and sneering Commissioner Saffino. The first was Sicilian, the other Piedmontese. They represented opposite worlds, and yet worked for the same master, with diverging methods and sensibilities.

The difference between them was best demonstrated in the captain's habit of addressing everyone formally, even if he was speaking to a fifteen-year-old boy. The commissioner, on the other hand, used the familiar form to address women, the elderly, and children, anyone from zero to one hundred years old.

When the captain entered your house, it was the state itself entering; the evil that had to be done for the supreme good that he served was delivered without pretense. The commissioner arrived with a smile on his face, delivering slaps on the back and criticizing the government, going on about how we were all friends, sitting down to eat and drink, and leaving happily, having bugged your bedroom or the table where he sat. But he loved everyone.

For both of them, we represented the enemy to be taken down by any means, even if it meant breaking the rules. The captain broke rules only if absolutely necessary, and with disgust. The commissioner loved to screw you over any way he could.

One of them, however, saw us as people. The other saw only scum.

They tried for months to get us out of the way legally: continuous searches, bugs everywhere, cameras. It was a permanent siege, in spite of the fact our area was peaceful. The bloodletting had ended, as had the Blood Brothers' harassment of civilians. But they couldn't stand that we were the ones who governed and imposed order.

They'll wear themselves out, we thought, and we patiently endured. Abruptly the siege ended and a period of apparent normality set in. But one night some time later, a shepherd who lived in a small neighboring district woke us up. A procession of vehicles was headed for the village.

This wasn't a raid. There were too many of them.

So the men left their beds and took refuge in the woods.

When we read the precautionary custody order, which was directed at all of us and about fifty friends of ours scattered throughout neighboring regions, we understood that the commissioner had had a stroke of genius.

Since his bugs hadn't picked up any confessions from us, he'd decided to bug our enemies. He filled the Blood Brothers' cars and houses with sophisticated electronic ears. The gangsters, who were unimaginably loquacious and oblivious to their audience, somehow rendered all the details of our sins while coincidentally managing to avoid disclosing a single incriminating detail about themselves.

The policemen filled notebooks with transcripts that blamed us for every evil that had occurred in the region.

Only our small group escaped prison; the surrounding

villages had been swept clean of our friends. The Blood Brothers quickly recovered their lost positions. But our freedom, albeit as fugitives, allowed us to avoid a bloody retaliation.

When the trial began, the presiding judge was the honorable Barresi, great-grandson of the illustrious Giovanni Andrea, who was still enjoying the fruits cultivated by Crocco the brigand.

Everything ran at an unusually fast pace; the upright judge dismantled any attempts on the part of the defense, and dictated the proceedings as though there was no choice but to deliver the maximum penalties.

We had a friend among the popular judges who updated us on the chamber discussions that took place after each hearing. There was no escape this time; we were scum who had to be erased from a society of which we were not worthy.

The defense attorneys defected one after the other, and the few brave souls who tried to point out the court's bias were branded as conniving accomplices—obstacles to justice.

Requests for appraisals and testimonies were rejected immediately, with no discussions in the council chamber. It was a farce.

In the end, unable to hang us as his ancestors had, Barresi handed down a few life sentences and a few others ranging from twenty to thirty years. Justice was served.

If they'd captured us, there would have been no hope for any of our friends.

We had to react and we took an unconventional approach.

We got out the *carabinieri* uniforms that poor Alfio had brought us and went to greet the champions of justice.

Despite the fact that the newspapers had been filled with reports of death threats looming over their persons and their loved ones, the protectors of public good lived peacefully in their beautiful homes. Aside from the occasional poor beat cop, no high representative of the institutions ever suffered any real danger. The state and its sham antagonism allowed them to sleep soundly.

The doors of the Barresi and Saffino households were opened without suspicion; they saw the uniforms and not the people who wore them. The judge and the commissioner soon found themselves locked in the trunks of two cars on an arduous drive through the mountains.

Luciano dusted off the acronym he'd coined so many years earlier in an attempt to save Rino's socialist friends. The elusive LAL, Locri Liberation Army, issued a leaflet addressed to the press in which they demanded, in exchange for the release of the two hostages, the freedom of our imprisoned friends and a review of their trials.

It was a desperate move, but it was the last card we could throw down in a game we'd been forced to play in the open. I was ready to pay the consequences for it.

We restored what had been Leonardo's cage all those years ago, back when men were swine, and we shoved the two whining heroes inside.

The state activated its every means, turning the country-side and neighboring villages upside down. But it would have taken years of searching this way to find the hostages, and they didn't have years. They needed a quick victory to stop the dangerous epidemic from spreading. There was only one way to do it: by negotiating.

They offered us piles of money. And we sent back their messengers with bins full of the cash from Milan that we'd buried nearby.

The state got the message, and the true negotiations began.

The armies of *carabinieri* that had been terrorizing our streets disappeared; the press was silenced. Elderly Marshal Palamita was left alone to patrol this patch of countryside. After this last assignment, a pension and his father's land in the Agrigentino were waiting for him. We saw him every-where in his old Campagnola. They'd certainly chosen the best messenger, perhaps the only one who could have gotten through to us.

He arrived early one morning, left the car far away and walked to the caves of Malupassu. I found him in the shade of a holm oak, where he had already been waiting for some time. He spoke aloud to the woods, not to me. ". . . Your father, old Bino, Sante, Santoro, the list goes on—how many more do you want to sacrifice? Do you feel like a fucking hero? It's time to end it, salvage what you can. You can talk to Captain Randone. He's a man who keeps his promises and only makes promises he can keep. I'll bring him to the mountains."

He didn't allow for an answer. He got up and left.

In a sense he was one of us, too, and he spoke for us.

After a week, the old *carabiniere* showed up with his boss on the peak above the caves of Malupassu. He showed Randone to a seat, then made as if to leave.

"You're in this shit, too, Rosario Palamita," I said, blocking him. Randone nodded and Palamita went to sit next to the captain.

The business was concluded in a matter of minutes. When it was done, we conversed for a few hours more. After all, I had spent years with Palamita, each of us on his own side. He reminisced about those years, until his superior made him understand that they had to leave.

I returned to the guys happy. "In a few months they'll start the appeals, you'll see."

A few days later, a squadron of soldiers discovered where the judge and the commissioner were being kept and freed the hostages; the state had won, as always. The kidnappers had managed to escape, but they'd soon be found.

The two freed martyrs of justice issued effusive declarations about how much they'd suffered to serve the common good. But of course they were not afraid, they wouldn't back down, they'd go on with their work. They described their imprisonment in minute detail, but couldn't describe their jailers, who were always hooded and seldom spoke. They were low-lifes who only cared about money.

Saffino was promoted and transferred so he could bring order to Valle d'Aosta. Judge Barresi's long imprisonment had exacerbated his health problems, and he was soon forced to leave his legal codes in the library and retire.

Then the story went silent.

The appeals process began. Fortunately for the defendants, the magistrates declared that most of the evidence obtained was inadmissible. There were many acquittals, and the few sentences they did hand down—to Luciano, Gino, Ciccio, Giulio, and me—were limited to a few short years.

We awaited the appellate court's decision in peace, the cops forgot about us, and we went back to sleeping in our homes.

I watched as the twins grew and Giulia's belly swelled again. The boys got married, one by one; even a blushing Tonino announced his engagement. Only Luciano held out against the bliss of family life. It was true happiness, unlike anything we'd ever felt before.

I hoped the confirmation process would take as long as possible, and I got my wish. The judges in Rome took over a year to finalize the sentences.

We had to honor our agreement with Randone.

We hugged each other with happiness and I set off with Luciano, Ciccio, Gino, and Giulio. The place we'd chosen for the state's final triumph was a farmhouse in the heart of the mountains; we arrived in the evening and waited until dawn for the Benemérita to come break down the doors.

The boys, tired from our walk, slept like angels, dreaming of their chaste fiancées. I wasn't tired and sat outside to enjoy the scenery. Spring had arrived overnight, the starry sky invited contemplation, and a warm breeze caressed the trees.

Luciano joined me. After forty years of telepathic communication between us, he suddenly felt it necessary to speak. After a few false starts, his deep voice pervaded the silence. His words took the form of a kind of thank you. He told me that he'd finally been able sleep during the past few months; he was no longer woken by the nightmare of his father surrounded by crows. He had quiet, normal dreams. He also wanted to tell me that Giulia was having another boy.

We felt no melancholy and spent the entire night recounting the brightest moments of our lives. Uncle Bino's stories, Luigi's amorous adventures, Tonino's brawls, the healthy ignorance of the boys who slept soundly inside.

At dawn we embraced, at peace with ourselves; the demon that had enslaved us for decades had abandoned us in search of new victims. Luciano asked me to make him coffee, and was taking one last drag on his second cigarette when the army of the state shattered our placid scene.

Roaring, ultramodern vehicles spat out armed boys in camouflage—kids who had come prepared to fight evil, after years of training. But instead of evil, all they found were two relaxed forty-year-olds in the mood for reminiscing. From the only older vehicle, a Campagnola, Palamita and Randone jumped out to curb the impetuous troops, relegating the mass of muscles to wait inside the huge off-road vehicles.

I made coffee for our guests and we woke the boys, who calmly started to get ready.

Despite his official duties, even Rosario allowed himself to be swept away by our memories. The officers sipped their coffee, while Luciano took advantage of the delay to smoke another cigarette. The marshal shared one story after the next, recounting our exploits to his superior, who despite his role and the task at hand often burst into fits of laughter. He chuckled with gusto at the description of the terrified *picciotto* whom Palamita had found near our goat enclosure one morning, and who with great embarrassment had showed him the contents of the sack he was carrying: the magnificent pair of horns that Sante Motta had sent to Don Peppino Zacco.

The soldiers in the off-road vehicles looked on in shock. They'd spent years on target practice and martial arts, and now, right before their eyes, an old man and a pudgy marshal were taming the cruelest brigands with inside jokes. Someone must have made a mistake. Where was the action they'd trained for? Where was the bloody battle that justified their extra pay?

Palamita went on undaunted, while our boys and the soldiers camped out under the trees to escape what felt like an August sun.

Then Palamita's voice began to falter. He mouthed words uselessly, became incomprehensible. The captain silenced him gently. He summoned the platoon and had our boys handcuffed one at a time, collected and loaded into a vehicle and driven off.

Giulio, Gino, and Ciccio said their warm goodbyes before their transports disappeared around the hairpin curves that descended into the valley.

Luciano and I stayed back with Randone, Palamita, and the units from a few of the last jeeps in the clearing in front of the farmhouse.

Luciano offered me his last good wishes, allowed himself to be handcuffed and, sandwiched by two giants, walked to the off-road vehicle that awaited him.

He was about to climb inside when he stopped suddenly and turned, catching the soldiers off guard.

He saw the captain grip my hand in a kind of salute instead of handcuffing me. Their eyes met, and he understood.

The agreement did not include prison time for me. That was not the promise I had made to secure my friends' futures. The state needed to have a complete victory. I was the one morally responsible for my companions' mistaken destinies; I was the one who would pay the price that had to be paid so that they could embark on new lives. It was the morality of the Aspromonte.

An animal howl, like a beast in agony, erupted from his depths, while the soldiers restrained him.

"Kyria!"

Kyria only gave him a tender smile and walked to the center of the clearing.

An incredible thunder shattered the cloudless sky; Kyria turned away and Luciano saw the hole in the nape of his neck, big enough to put a fist through, vomiting blood and brain matter.

Kyria turned back to Luciano and the soldiers and smiled again; it was nothing, he was fine, he could walk with his own legs.

Luciano thought about how Kyria had never smiled like that in his life. He thought of him as a child, back when they'd watch Zacco pass and his eyes shone with a hellish fire.

Randone approached to help support Luciano.

Kyria stepped toward Rosario Palamita, who had covered his face with his hand. He wanted to apologize for splattering the marshal with slime, but the marshal was the only man he would have allowed to do the job.

Rosario was from the mountains, too, mountains far from the Aspromonte but not so different. He was the only one who had fought fair and who hadn't seen his opponents as beasts; he'd performed that last act out of duty.

Rosario had worn the uniform of the Benemérita with pride his entire life, but that day his clothes felt fetid and heavy, and he wanted to shed them right then and there.

Kyria stood opposite him. "It didn't hurt," he said, and then his gaze grew distant.

He saw a splendid valley, a placid body of water at the foot of a proud hill, thriving cattle and goats at pasture. Paradise.

And then he saw them.

First old Bino, then his father, then Sante and little Santoro. And behind them, an ancient and familiar warrior, Kyria. They'd all shared the same dream.

His muscles went slack and he collapsed into Rosario's arms.

ABOUT THE AUTHOR

Gioacchino Criaco was born in Africo, a small town on the Ionian coast of Calabria. The son of Aspromonte shepherds, Criaco graduated from the University of Bologna with a degree in law and practiced as a lawyer in Milan until 2008, when his debut novel, *Anime Nere* (*Black Souls*), was published to great international acclaim. Since then, Criaco has published five other novels and overseen the adaptation of *Black Souls* into a prize-winning film. He divides his time between Milan and Calabria.

EDITOR'S NOTES

PART I

"Wrinkle of humanity . . ." (13): In 1951, the people of Africo, the town where Gioacchino Criaco was born, were relocated from high in the Aspromonte massif, a secluded densely forested area described as a seven hours' march from the next nearest town. The reason for the removal of the population was, ostensibly, the people's safety, as the "old town" had suffered several disastrous floods. However, there is much more to the story, as Africo had become a political bugaboo; in 1948, *L'Europeo* journalist Tommaso Besozzi had profiled the city as being an "emblem of desperation," Africo became a poster child of Southern Italian poverty.

The residents of Africo, who numbered about three thousand, had been living in that harsh, inaccessible, and idyllic mountain forest for more than a thousand years. The evacuated population was relocated to a "new city" that was carved out of Bianco, an existing municipality by the coast, but through various bureaucratic delays and political setbacks the new city by the sea was not ready for the Africoti until 1963. During the twelve years between evacuation and resettlement, the people of Africo lived in temporary refugee structures around Reggio Calabria—dispossessed of their homes, their millennium-old way of life, their mountains. In this period of turmoil, many young men resorted to emigration or to organized crime for their livelihood.

Criaco himself was born in the new city by the sea after the evacuation. Like many Africoti, Criaco describes a yearning for the mountain home he never knew, and his characters divide their time between the coastal new city and their clandestine excursions to the mountains they were supposed to have left behind. The narrator uses the term "the wrinkle," *la ruga* in the original Italian, to refer to the urban block he grows up in in his city by the sea, in contrast to his father's fold in the mountains, where the sons of goatherds find refuge in the remnants of a lifestyle from which they have been torn away.

"In those years, in addition to the infamous kidnappings . . ." (15): In the 1970s, the 'Ndrangehta, which had largely managed to keep a much lower profile than Italy's other mafias, started to make national and international news on a daily basis through a series of kidnappings. One of the most famous instances was the kidnapping of John Paul Getty III, the teenage heir of the Getty oil business, who was kidnapped in 1973 and held for five months, during which time he almost died. But there were many other instances of brutal and occasionally fatal kidnappings.

Tingiùto (17): Literally, tinged; darkened by coal.

"Of the shadows who stayed with us during the war . . ." (18): The First 'Ndrangheta War, as it has been labeled, was a bloody internal war that lasted from 1974–1976 and resulted in the deaths of at least 233 made men.

Malandrino/i (17): Literally, crook. Criaco uses the word to refer to a member of a local 'ndrina (as 'Ndrangheta cells are called).

"On account of his sister, my father was not, nor could he ever have become, a malandrino himself . . ." (19): Since the 1920s, the 'Ndrangheta has had very strict rules about membership. A man cannot join if a woman in his immediate family has ever been a prostitute; other sexual purity laws, which the narrative addresses later, require exclusion of men who have been cuckolded or who are the product of cuckolding. Nor can a man join if any member of his immediate family has ever been on a police force.

picciotto/i (37): Literally "young guys," or as John Dickie has translated, "lads with attitude." The entry-level ranking in the 'Ndrangheta once a young man has gone through the blood oath ceremony; an equivalent in other mafias would be a soldier.

"Tell my friend Peppino I had a son who I named after his late friend . . ." (37): When Santino says "his late friend," he is referencing his own murdered father. His intent is clear because of Calabrese naming conventions that dictate a man names his son after his own father (the child's paternal grandfather). Santino's statement also clearly implies that he knows Don Peppino was involved in his father's murder.

"If he wants to honor us with his presence . . ." (37): 'Ndrangheta protocol historically insisted on politeness and formal language, even in a case like this one, where Sante is threatening Don Peppino via a lowly messenger.

"Because my friend," he said, "is cursed by the evil eye" (38): As Peppino and Santino gift each other with goat horns—*cornetti*, which are widely used in Calabria to protect against the evil eye, including in effigy as horn-shaped gold charms worn on chains—they are also mutually insulting each other, since a *cornutto*, or a "horned one," is Calabrese slang for a cuckold.

carabiniere (76): Italy has several major police forces. The *carabinieri* are a federal force, a branch of the military, but are responsible for local beat cop work. To prevent corruption, *carabinieri* are never stationed in the region of Italy they are from. Rosario Palamita, a native Sicilian, is the long-standing *carabinieri* assigned to the narrator's region of the Aspromonte.

"That wouldn't have been the first time Luciano had jinxed us with his comments . . ." (48): The Italian original calls Luciano "*grillo parlante*," or talking cricket, an allusion to the talking cricket in Carlo Collodi's *Pinocchio*. In the story, the talking cricket is killed by Pinocchio for offering him unwanted advice, then later comes back as a ghost to continue to offer advice Pinocchio ignores.

"They called us the 'children of the forest,' we descendants of the people who had inhabited the woods of the Calabrian massif for millennia . . ." (53): Africo was not the only Aspromonte town that was evacuated to the coast during the 20th century. Two of the most famous, both of them now tourist attractions as ghost towns, are Pentedattilo, from the Greek for "Five Fingers," which was abandoned in the 1960s, and Roghudi, which was abandoned in 1973. But the peaks and washes of the Aspromonte massif are dotted with empty villages.

"Who had begun to refer to all northerners as Piedmontese after Garibaldi came through . . ." (56): In August 1962, Giuseppe Garibaldi, hero general of Italian unification, led an army of two thousand volunteers into the Aspromonte on a march that was meant to take them from Sicily to Rome to challenge the Pope's rule of the Papal States, which Garibaldi believed should be incorporated in Italy. However, Garibaldi was mistaken in thinking the Kingdom of Italy government supported this endeavor, and his volunteers were stopped in the mountains by royal troops.

PART II

"The feast of San Silvestro" (64): December 31. The feast day of Saint Sylvester, an early 4th century pope, is celebrated throughout Italy, but the saint is especially revered in Calabria, where he is said to have traveled, including in some traditions in the company of the Emperor Constantine.

"We were retracing the steps of the Saint, the protector . . ." (70): Although Criaco never names the saint in question here, the text is referring to Saint Leo of Bova, the saint dearest to Africo and several other Aspromonte villages (although not, it should be noted, the town's patron saint, who is Saint Rocco). Saint Leo is an obscure saint whose legacy has been almost entirely lost. He was born in the ninth or tenth century in Bova, and after joining the ascetic Basilian monastic order, came deep into the Aspromonte to pray in the icy waters near Africo. He arrived during a period of famine and presented the starving locals with pine pitch, which miraculously transformed into bread when they took it home. His feast day is still celebrated with an annual pilgrimage up to his church in abandoned Africo Vecchio.

"Whom we began to call Salvatore, or Sasà for short" (116): The name Salvatore, literally "savior," can be found throughout Italy but is most concentrated in the South. Here, in addition to the implications of its definition, the boys are christening him with a tongue-in-cheek honorary for someone from their region, similar, in the US, to calling him an all-American Joe or Tom, but with the added regional layer of a Huck or a Tucker.

PART III

"We filled the lanes with our powerful cars, crisscrossing the peninsula and the continent . . ." (123): Calabria has been one of the regions of Italy hardest hit by emigration. Due to a combination of factors—abject poverty, feudal exploitation, predatory landlordism, oppressive taxes on regional industries (particularly goats, which are so important in *Black Souls*), and uneven industrial development in the North—millions of Calabrians have departed their home in search of work, temporarily or permanently, in the Americas, Australia, Germany, France, and the cities of northern Italy.

PART IV

"the saint-burners" (169): Made men of the 'Ndrangheta; 'Ndranghetisti. Part of the 'Ndrangheta initiation rite includes holding a burning image of a saint in your hand until it is ash while repeating the initiation formulas.

"the Gozzini law" (174): In 1986, a prison reform law was passed. It included holiday leave for prisoners and the opportunity to reduce sentences in the event of good behavior.

"Sirens accompanied us all the way to the Fatebenefratelli . . ." (194): Fatebenefratelli, in actuality the name of a large Milan hospital, is here used as Milanese slang for central booking.

PART V

"We were happy with our black bread . . ." (224): In 1928, when the journalist and social activist Umberto Zanotti

Bianco visited Africo, he was horrified to see the impover-ished residents lived off an unwholesome (in his opinion) bread made of lentils and acorns. The black bread of the Aspromonte became one of the symbols of Africo's poverty, which later caused it to be labeled "the poorest, the saddest" village in Calabria by Tommaso Besozzi.

"Saffino was promoted and transferred so he could bring order to Valle d'Aosta . . ." (252): A cushy transfer to one of Italy's wealthiest and least populated regions.

Other Titles in the Soho Crime Series

Stephanie Barron
(Jane Austen's England)
*Jane and the Twelve Days
of Christmas*
Jane and the Waterloo Map

F.H. Batacan
(Philippines)
Smaller and Smaller Circles

James R. Benn
(World War II Europe)
Billy Boyle
The First Wave
Blood Alone
Evil for Evil
Rag & Bone
A Mortal Terror
Death's Door
A Blind Goddess
The Rest Is Silence
The White Ghost
Blue Madonna
The Devouring
Solemn Graves
When Hell Struck Twelve

Cara Black
(Paris, France)
Murder in the Marais
Murder in Belleville
Murder in the Sentier
Murder in the Bastille
Murder in Clichy
Murder in Montmartre
*Murder on the
Ile Saint-Louis*
*Murder in the
Rue de Paradis*
Murder in the Latin Quarter
Murder in the Palais Royal
Murder in Passy
*Murder at the
Lanterne Rouge*
*Murder Below
Montparnasse*
Murder in Pigalle

Cara Black cont.
*Murder on the
Champ de Mars*
Murder on the Quai
Murder in Saint-Germain
Murder on the Left Bank
Murder in Bel-Air

Lisa Brackmann
(China)
Rock Paper Tiger
Hour of the Rat
Dragon Day

Getaway
Go-Between

Henry Chang
(Chinatown)
Chinatown Beat
Year of the Dog
Red Jade
Death Money
Lucky

Barbara Cleverly
(England)
The Last Kashmiri Rose
Strange Images of Death
The Blood Royal
Not My Blood
A Spider in the Cup
Enter Pale Death
Diana's Altar

Fall of Angels
Invitation to Die

Colin Cotterill
(Laos)
The Coroner's Lunch
Thirty-Three Teeth
Disco for the Departed
Anarchy and Old Dogs
Curse of the Pogo Stick
The Merry Misogynist
*Love Songs from
a Shallow Grave*
Slash and Burn

Colin Cotterill cont.
*The Woman Who
Wouldn't Die*
*Six and a
Half Deadly Sins*
I Shot the Buddha
The Rat Catchers' Olympics
Don't Eat Me
The Second Biggest Nothing

Garry Disher
(Australia)
The Dragon Man
Kittyhawk Down
Snapshot
Chain of Evidence
Blood Moon
Whispering Death
Signal Loss

Wyatt
Port Vila Blues
Fallout

Bitter Wash Road
Under the Cold Bright Lights

David Downing
(World War II Germany)
Zoo Station
Silesian Station
Stettin Station
Potsdam Station
Lehrter Station
Masaryk Station

(World War I)
Jack of Spies
One Man's Flag
Lenin's Roller Coaster
The Dark Clouds Shining
*Diary of a Dead Man
on Leave*

Agnete Friis
(Denmark)
What My Body Remembers
The Summer of Ellen

Michael Genelin
(Slovakia)
Siren of the Waters
Dark Dreams
The Magician's Accomplice
Requiem for a Gypsy

Timothy Hallinan
(Thailand)
The Fear Artist
For the Dead
The Hot Countries
Fools' River

(Los Angeles)
Crashed
Little Elvises
The Fame Thief
Herbie's Game
King Maybe
Fields Where They Lay
Nighttown

Mette Ivie Harrison
(Mormon Utah)
The Bishop's Wife
His Right Hand
For Time and All Eternities
Not of This Fold

Mick Herron
(England)
Slow Horses
Dead Lions
Real Tigers
Spook Street
London Rules
Joe Country

Down Cemetery Road
The Last Voice You Hear
Why We Die
Smoke and Whispers

Reconstruction
Nobody Walks
This Is What Happened

Stan Jones
(Alaska)
White Sky, Black Ice
Shaman Pass

Stan Jones cont.
Frozen Sun
Village of the Ghost Bears
Tundra Kill
The Big Empty

**Lene Kaaberbøl &
Agnete Friis**
(Denmark)
The Boy in the Suitcase
Invisible Murder
Death of a Nightingale
The Considerate Killer

Martin Limón
(South Korea)
Jade Lady Burning
Slicky Boys
Buddha's Money
The Door to Bitterness
The Wandering Ghost
G.I. Bones
Mr. Kill
The Joy Brigade
Nightmare Range
The Iron Sickle
The Ville Rat
Ping-Pong Heart
The Nine-Tailed Fox
The Line
GI Confidential

Ed Lin
(Taiwan)
Ghost Month
Incensed
99 Ways to Die

Peter Lovesey
(England)
The Circle
The Headhunters
False Inspector Dew
Rough Cider
On the Edge
The Reaper

(Bath, England)
The Last Detective
Diamond Solitaire
The Summons

Peter Lovesey cont.
Bloodhounds
Upon a Dark Night
The Vault
Diamond Dust
The House Sitter
The Secret Hangman
Skeleton Hill
Stagestruck
Cop to Corpse
The Tooth Tattoo
The Stone Wife
*Down Among
the Dead Men*
Another One Goes Tonight
Beau Death
Killing with Confetti

(London, England)
Wobble to Death
*The Detective Wore
Silk Drawers*
Abracadaver
Mad Hatter's Holiday
The Tick of Death
A Case of Spirits
Swing, Swing Together
Waxwork

Jassy Mackenzie
(South Africa)
Random Violence
Stolen Lives
The Fallen
Pale Horses
Bad Seeds

Sujata Massey
(1920s Bombay)
The Widows of Malabar Hill
The Satapur Moonstone

Francine Mathews
(Nantucket)
Death in the Off-Season
Death in Rough Water
Death in a Mood Indigo
Death in a Cold Hard Light
Death on Nantucket

Seichō Matsumoto
(Japan)
Inspector Imanishi
Investigates

Magdalen Nabb
(Italy)
Death of an Englishman
Death of a Dutchman
Death in Springtime
Death in Autumn
The Marshal and
the Murderer
The Marshal and
the Madwoman
The Marshal's Own Case
The Marshal Makes
His Report
The Marshal
at the Villa Torrini
Property of Blood
Some Bitter Taste
The Innocent
Vita Nuova
The Monster of Florence

Fuminori Nakamura
(Japan)
The Thief
Evil and the Mask
Last Winter, We Parted
The Kingdom
The Boy in the Earth
Cult X

Stuart Neville
(Northern Ireland)
The Ghosts of Belfast
Collusion
Stolen Souls
The Final Silence
Those We Left Behind
So Say the Fallen

(Dublin)
Ratlines

Rebecca Pawel
(1930s Spain)
Death of a Nationalist
Law of Return
The Watcher in the Pine
The Summer Snow

Kwei Quartey
(Ghana)
Murder at Cape
Three Points
Gold of Our Fathers
Death by His Grace

Qiu Xiaolong
(China)
Death of a Red Heroine
A Loyal Character Dancer
When Red Is Black

James Sallis
(New Orleans)
The Long-Legged Fly
Moth
Black Hornet
Eye of the Cricket
Bluebottle
Ghost of a Flea

Sarah Jane

John Straley
(Sitka, Alaska)
The Woman Who
Married a Bear
The Curious Eat Themselves
The Music of What Happens
Death and the Language
of Happiness
The Angels Will Not Care
Cold Water Burning
Baby's First Felony

(Cold Storage, Alaska)
The Big Both Ways
Cold Storage, Alaska

Akimitsu Takagi
(Japan)
The Tattoo Murder Case
Honeymoon to Nowhere
The Informer

Helene Tursten
(Sweden)
Detective Inspector Huss
The Torso
The Glass Devil
Night Rounds
The Golden Calf
The Fire Dance
The Beige Man
The Treacherous Net
Who Watcheth
Protected by the Shadows

Hunting Game
Winter Grave

An Elderly Lady Is Up to
No Good

Janwillem van de
Wetering
(Holland)
Outsider in Amsterdam
Tumbleweed
The Corpse on the Dike
Death of a Hawker
The Japanese Corpse
The Blond Baboon
The Maine Massacre
The Mind-Murders
The Streetbird
The Rattle-Rat
Hard Rain
Just a Corpse at Twilight
Hollow-Eyed Angel
The Perfidious Parrot
The Sergeant's Cat:
Collected Stories

Jacqueline Winspear
(1920s England)
Maisie Dobbs
Birds of a Feather